SPIRIT OF IRON

HARWOOD STEELE

Made with ♥ on the Notion Press Platform
www.notionpress.com

Contents

"Spirit-of-Iron" is an attempt to present fact in the form of romantic fiction. It portrays the development of North-Western Canada in the pioneer period, the main events of which, with one or two exceptions, have been closely followed.

The characters are types. Hector Adair is intended to represent the ideal Mounted Police officer in particular and the ideal British officer generally. He is not to be identified with any historical figure connected with the Force. The plan, here employed, of symbolizing and tracing the development of a country through the development of an individual such as Hector is, I think, new. The politician, Welland, similarly, is a type, and has no definite connection with any famous politician of real life. The men of the Police—the Marquis, Sergeant Kellett and others—are also types, true to the extraordinary calibre of the Force. The remaining characters—whom the reader may identify if—and as—he chooses, all had their originals in the old Canadian North-West.

Practically every incident and episode of the story had its origin in fact. The arrest of Wild Horse, the Whitewash Bill man-hunt, the holding of Hopeful Pass and innumerable minor incidents all occurred, though not necessarily in the circumstances described, while the details of the dangerous plot confronting Hector in Book IV are drawn, almost line for line, from a great if obscure page in the more recent history of the Mounted Police in the North. Hector's long struggle with Welland is not based on any particular conflict of this kind in real life, but that such things occur, in Canada as elsewhere, any man acquainted with the Services and politics can vouch for. Finally, the locale of each episode is not necessarily to be identified with any particular point in our North-West.

The word "Royal" is everywhere omitted from the title of the Force because the honourary distinction of "Royal" was not theirs when the events covered in this novel took place.

I have described the book as "An Authentic Novel of the North-West Mounted Police" because I wish to emphasize that it endeavours to present the Force as it was and is and not as portrayed by well-meaning but ignorant writers of the "red love, two-gun" variety, and it is my hope that, through this book, the reader may obtain a clearer conception of the marvellous devotion to duty, the high idealism, the splendid efficiency which have made the Mounted Police famous than any to be derived from these inaccurate romances.

HARWOOD STEELE.

1

BOOK ONE: On the Anvil

———•♡•———

The time had come for the North-West Mounted Police to say goodbye to Lower Fort Garry, the home of the Force since its inception some months before.

In the clear spring dawn, the scarlet-coated column fell in, ranging behind it a long tail of ox-carts and wagons. Sergeant-Major Whittaker, of 'J' Division, a straight-backed, dapper, sinewy little man with a pair of fierce moustaches, called the roll. The Regimental Sergeant-Major, trotting over to the bearded Assistant-Commissioner, reported all ready to march. Orders cracked down the line. With a shout, a thunder of hoofs and the roll of heavy wheels, the cavalcade surged into motion.

In the rear of the column rode Constable Hector Adair.

II

A fine, big, handsome fellow, Hector, a splendid specimen of what the Province of Ontario could produce when it tried, and looking every inch what he was—the son of a hardy soldier-father, that Colonel Adair who had been one of the pioneers of old Blenheim County, at home, and who, before that, had served under the Iron Duke himself in the Peninsula and at Waterloo. This young giant's broad shoulders and deep chest would have been the envy of many heavy dragoons, and he was six feet tall. His face, bronzed, with straight nose, strong chin, firm mouth and steel-grey eyes, had in it a great power and yet an idealism unspoilt by contact with the rotten side of Life. Men—a keen observer felt—though knowing him still a boy—he was actually twenty—would regard him as a man, fear him intensely and follow him anywhere. Women would thrill at his physique, linger over his brown hair, know him a man, regard him as a boy and love him with a love largely maternal.

More than this, he looked the soldier-born. No finer school for the making of men ever existed than the old, partially developed Upper Canada where Hector had first seen the light and spent his childhood. It had been rough, crude and half civilized but also vigorous and strong. Its immense forests, its rapid streams, its solitudes possessed by dangerous wild animals, had given him resource, self-reliance, endurance, courage. The most ordinary affairs of life—a visit to the nearest settlement, the routine journey to church or school—tested the quality of many a grown man. The barest necessities were won only by the hardest of hard work. Even the pastimes of the district round about demanded much pluck and stamina. Blue blood went without luxuries and handled axe or plough. Men were men there, boys were men in miniature, and women were worthy of their sons and husbands—more could not be said in praise of them. Altogether, the natural environment which had been Hector's as a boy could not help but develop in him the first requisite of the born soldier—true manhood. And the sports to be enjoyed in Blenheim county—shooting, fishing, big game hunting in the heart of the great wildernesses—had made him a giant at last, with a heart that nothing shook and no nerves whatever.

If all this were not enough, Hector's boyhood associates had been of a character which must inevitably have shaped him into what he was. Take the Colonel, who, coming out to Canada to occupy land under one of the earliest settlement schemes, had built up prosperity for himself and constructed Silvercrest, his fine estate, from the trackless wild. The Colonel, from the first, had intended that his son should have a Commission in the Army and carry on the fighting traditions of a martial family. He believed, besides, in King Solomon's adage concerning the rod and the spoiled child, considered that boys should be seldom seen and never heard and held other ideas equally as uncomfortable.

The Colonel had not been able to spare much time to Hector, but, such as it was, it was well spent. He had not only thrashed him when he needed it, but had educated him. Knowing that the little country school could give his son only a rudimentary education, he expended an hour or so a day in teaching Hector many things in literature, geography, history and mathematics—particularly literature. By great effort, labouriously bringing many of the books all the way from England, the Colonel had formed a fine library at Silvercrest. The old classics were there, with later and contemporary writers—Scott, Coleridge, Dickens and Alfred Tennyson, the handsome lion of the Old Land. Father and son had toiled most studiously over these treasures and it was worth something to see the small, brown-haired boy struggling with the heroes of Greece under the stern eye of his white-haired parent. Hector had the run of the room and on rainy days all the giants of romance and chivalry took full possession of that book-lined haven in the wilderness. Such passages as this rang like far trumpets in his ears:

I made them lay their hands in mine and swear
To reverence the King as if he were
Their conscience and their conscience as their King;
To break the heathen and uphold the Christ,
To ride abroad redressing human wrongs,
To speak no slander, no, nor listen to it,
To honour his own word as if his God's,
To lead sweet lives in purest chastity,
To love one maiden only, cleave to her
And worship her by years of noble deeds
Until they won her....

These stirring lines, from the beginning, had filled him with strange longings and given him a great ideal.

Besides these more general things, much of the Colonel's teaching had been devoted to building up the boy into that splendid product, 'an officer and a gentleman.'

Then there was his mother—a sweet, gentle, dainty woman, of marvellous housekeeping ability. From her, Hector had learned such of those fine, old-fashioned principles as the Colonel had been too busy to teach. Hector's little sister, Nora—his constant companion in his boyhood doings, rendering him profound homage and devotion and regarding him as a demigod, the mover of mountains, the achiever of impossibilities—had done much to make him chivalrous. His cousins Hugh and Allen, boys of his own age who lived close by, could not be said to have much influenced him, except to make him one of the most reckless lads and finest sportsmen in the county, though from his older cousin, John, he had learnt all he knew of woodcraft and athletics.

But the men on his father's farm had done more to make a soldier out of Hector than even the Colonel. They were all veterans of many campaigns, or at least members of the local militia—none but these were granted work at Silvercrest. Grey old, lean old Sergeant Pierce, the Colonel's right-hand man, had marched with the 28th, the Colonel's own Regiment, from Torres Vedras to the Pyrenees. Corporal Hardwick, late of the 95th, had served in the Kaffir Wars and accompanied the 'Green Jackets' in the attack on the Sevastapol Ovens. Private Toombs had aided the 57th—the famous 'Die-hards'—in suppressing the 'Sepoy Rebellion.' 'Maintop' MacEachern, senior naval representative, a lean, white-whiskered old sea-dog, had been a powder-monkey under Broke when the Shannon took the Chesapeake. And 'Long Dick' Masters, the 'daddy' of the whole crowd, barring Sergeant Pierce, and so tall that he could give even the Sergeant a couple of inches, had long ago led the rush of the York Volunteers at Queenston Heights.

The influence of such men on a youngster's development was inevitably potent. Thanks to them, Silvercrest had overflowed with Service tradition. As a small boy, Hector had been allowed to form them into a little company, which, under the Sergeant's supervision, he drilled with unflagging zeal, until he was as efficient as the smartest instructor in the smartest regiment of the Guards. They told him yarns of a hundred fights and fields. They sang him marvellous choruses—'Ranzo,' 'We'll Fight the Greeks and Romans on the High Seas-O,' 'The Bold Soldier Boy' and many others—which in their day had startled the French outposts in Spain or enlivened the fo'c's'le of the Victory. They gave him such formulæ as this, which he had from Sergeant Pierce: 'Don't knuckle down to a bully. Don't start the trouble but take on anything that breathes if there's good reason. Stand up to your man like a soldier, even if you know you're licked, and fight—d'you see, little master?—till the last shot's fired.' And, between them, they drove him wild to serve the Queen.

No wonder, then, that he rode out today in the midst of the Mounted Police.

But why was he only a ranker—when the Colonel, from the first, had trained him for a Commission?

Of this—a word later.

III

So the years of Hector's boyhood had been passed in an atmosphere of idealistic tradition.

His first attempt at soldiering in earnest was made when he was twelve years old—with the Fenian raids on the Niagara Peninsula.

The Blenheim Rangers, one of Upper Canada's finest militia regiments, being called out on this occasion to defend the frontier, Hector yearned to march away with them. He thought, poor youngster, that he might be allowed to serve as a bugler or a drummer, for he was big and strong for his age. Born, as Maintop put it, with a sword in his hand and epaulettes on his shoulders, accustomed all his life to hear of 'sallies and retires, of trenches, tents' and such matters, his daily course shaped with the idea that he was eventually to have a Commission, this was only natural. The Colonel, equally naturally, refused point-blank to let him go. And—again of course—Hector took the law into his own hands and ran away.

All was confusion and anxiety at Silvercrest during the following three days and a hue and cry sought Hector over half Upper Canada. When eventually he was brought back, a dishevelled, unhappy little figure, the Colonel found he had not the heart to punish him as he deserved. He could only gently reprove him and promise that, in any future emergency, provided the authorities would have him, he would be allowed to go.

Though Hector's share in the repulse of the Fenian raids was thus brought to nought, the attempt had at least shown that the spirit of soldiering was strong within him.

The Colonel's promise was tested and Hector's second opportunity came with the expedition sent to crush the rebellion on the Red River. The boy was then sixteen and already of fine physique. John, who had a Commission in one of the regiments, requested and, to Hector's rapture, received permission to enlist him in his company. But again Fate stepped in, cruelly. Hector got as far as Toronto, where the expedition was assembling, when a telegram recalled him. His adored little sister, Nora, always delicate, was dying of pneumonia caught in a summer storm. Hector reached home in time to hold her dead body in his arms. He was heart-broken. Grown pale and stooped and haggard in a night, his father made him a piteous appeal.

"Hector," he had said, "I want you to give up this idea of going to Fort Garry. It would have been different had—had Nora lived. But your mother needs you now. She can't lose her two babies at once. Everything can be arranged. My friends in the Rifles will give you your discharge. I hate to disappoint you a second time, boy. I'm asking you to make a big sacrifice."

And Hector—with a great effort of real courage—had answered quietly,

"Of course, in that case, sir—I'll not go."

So he moved a step nearer true manhood.

IV

At Toronto, while waiting to go to Red River, Hector had a strange experience—an isolated thing, as incongruous as a wreath of flowers in the mouth of a cannon. He had not, at that time, the perception to realize that it was the first shadow of things to come, sent to open his eyes to his dawning power.

One evening, walking by himself, he struck up an acquaintance with a young fellow named George Harris. Afterwards, they saw each other frequently. Hector enjoyed George's company, because he was refreshingly unlike any other boy he had ever met, an amazing complexity, made up of many extremes. He had odd fits of melancholy, when he said nothing, alternating with bursts of liveliness, when he chattered away for hours on any subject. Though he neither smoked nor drank, he could swear with marvellous fluency—like a schoolboy in the role of man-about-town. Possessed of an extraordinary eye for a well-dressed woman or a handsome man, he yet hated Hector to look at either. He had rooms in town, but persistently refused to ask Hector into them. No persuasion would induce him to go out except at night. Altogether, he was a curious fellow.

Then came the revelation. The childish side of George's character showed itself one evening in enthusiastic declarations that he wished he was a soldier. Hector agreed it was a fine life. That fairly launched George. Real soldiering did not appeal to him. It was the glamour of display—the great reviews, the bands, the gleaming scarlet.

Quite carried away, he halted in the street, clasped his hands and exclaimed ecstatically:

"Oh, I love to hear the jingling of the spurs!"

Instantly Hector's suspicions, till then stupidly dormant, had flamed up. He glanced around the dark street. No-one was in sight. They were in the bright glow of a lamp.

Sending George's hat spinning, he caught him by the wrists in a fierce grip. And—a mass of fair hair came tumbling down the captive's shoulders—a pretty face, distorted with alarm, sprang into view—

A girl! All the moods and caprices were instantly explained. A girl!

Hector's heart beat furiously. He held her tight.

"Let me go!" she gasped, struggling. "You're hurting me. We'll be seen! Let me go!"

Hector flamed into frightened rage—he was very young and knew nothing of women.

"Who are you?" he panted. "What do you mean by it? Supposing we'd been caught like this? You fool—you fool!—"

"Let me go!" she begged.

"Answer me, will you?" he stormed.

Realizing that this was a woman several years older than himself, he became suddenly conscious of his helplessness in her hands and felt something not far from terror seize him.

"What am I to think of you?"

"Shut up!" White, with agonized tears in her eyes, she looked defiantly into his face. "I won't have you talk to me like this. Oh, I know I've run the risk of ruining myself and hurting you, but I don't care—no, I don't! I'm just as straight as—as—" She mastered herself with an effort. "Listen! Do you think I'd have dressed myself up like this otherwise? Gone to all this trouble? And taken these chances? And kept you out of my rooms? You bet I wouldn't! I'd have dressed myself up to kill and stopped you on the street. But a—a straight girl can't do that! So I had to do this. It was the only way. Oh, can't you see?"

"Had to! The only way!"

Bitter scorn lashed her.

"Yes, it was," she said. Suddenly she dropped her voice and turned her face to his. "I saw you out walking several times. I had to know you. Hector, don't you understand?"

He was dazed. He clung to her wrists.

"You fool—" she went on, with a strange little laugh. "You are the fool, funny, silly boy! Don't you see—I'm mad about you, Hector?"

This frightened him more than ever.

"The devil you are!" he ground out. "Who are you, anyway? What am I going to do to you?"

Desperately humiliated, she fought to escape. He held her strongly. She gasped and prayed for release but he would not listen.

"Hector," she had implored, at last, "if you're a gentleman—if you've any sense of chivalry—!"

Any sense of chivalry? She had struck the right note.

He let her go—watched her run away until the night swallowed her. Then, in a sort of stupour, he picked up his swagger stick and walked back to his quarters....

Nothing in his experience, before or since, had so closely resembled a 'love affair.'

V

Strangely enough, it was to his father's death that Hector eventually owed his opportunity to achieve the life for which he had been trained since birth—life in the service of the Queen; and the realization of his boyhood dreams of chivalry.

To this, too, he owed the fact that, when eventually he donned the scarlet tunic, that tunic was, not the gold-laced vestment of an officer, but the plain coat of a ranker, in the Mounted Police.

The status under which he entered the Service was a heavy disappointment. His early enlistments in the militia or the Rifles for the Red River had been merely preliminary canters regarded at the time as useful training for the future Commission. Hector was not ashamed of his ranker's uniform. He knew the true worth of the man who carries the rifle and pack. Though the sword points the way, the bayonet must follow—or there can be no victory. But the high heart aspires to the sword rather than the bayonet. It is not always easy to follow. It is always difficult to lead. He wished to lead—had been trained and moulded for leadership. To have to relinquish leadership or give up the Service altogether had been a terrible blow to him—how terrible only those who come of Service blood and have lived for years in a Service atmosphere can really appreciate.

For to such as these—to such as Hector—the Army is no machine, no hide-bound association of slaves marching in the lockstep of brutal discipline; nor is it a great dramatic society devoted to meaningless ritual and pompous display. At its worst, it is not the raving monster of ignorant fancy, revelling in sacrifice and blood. But it is something so wonderful that no pen on earth can picture it. It is a glorious brotherhood, a religion giving and demanding much of its votaries—demanding dauntless devotion, iron endurance, inflexible loyalty to God, King, division, battalion—giving the knowledge of work well done and petty selfishness voluntarily set aside for the good of the common cause. To such as these there is marvellous music in the wild voice of the bugle—hallowed by sacred memories and age-old traditions—and the majestic dignity and power in the mere sight of a brigade presenting arms will bring a lump to their throats, while the Colours, tattered, stained with the blood of heroes, emblazoned with the names of great victories, have about them something almost divine. They have one mistress—these Service men—one mother, one sister, whose honour is in their hands and for whom they will die without a murmur. She watches them, rewards them, punishes them, loves them, guards them, from the 'Reveille' of their first morning to the 'Last Post' and three rounds blank of the last night of all. She is fair as the moon, clear as the sun, terrible as an army with banners. They call her The Regiment.

A place in this great brotherhood belongs to every soldier. But the officer is the High Priest of the order. It is for him to guide and encourage his men, to rally the broken line, halt the retreat, give fresh life to the failing charge and gather the spears into his breast to make a place for them to follow. Rob a boy trained for leadership of his birthright and he loses everything he considers worth while. Cut him off from The Regiment and—break his heart.

The Colonel had succumbed to a stroke. His fatal illness had not come suddenly. From the day of Nora's death, it had begun. Nora seemed to have taken away the Colonel's vigour with her. But the decline was not solely on her account. For years, though Hector had not known it till too late, the Colonel had laboured under a heavy financial burden—notes endorsed—bad harvests—family honour—the old, old story.

To this state of affairs, above everything, the change of plans for Hector's future had been due. The old gentleman had torn his heart out when he told his son that he must give up the idea of a Regular Commission or even of enlisting because it had become his duty to go into business and redeem the family fortune.

The hideous truth had revealed itself by slow degrees after the Colonel's death, when it was seen that practically nothing was left for Hector and his mother, that Silvercrest and everything in it must go, that Hector would have to get some kind of work at once and that Mrs. Adair must transfer herself to John's, for the time at least.

Came into Hector's hands, at this crisis, a clipping, like the blast of a trumpet sounding specially for him.

'Recruiting for New Police Force Commences,' said the headlines of the clipping. 'Officers in City.'

There followed a description of the measures which were about to enforce the new North-West Mounted Police Act. It seemed that three hundred men 'who should be mounted as the Government should from time to time direct,' were being assembled for duty as military constabulary in the North-West Territories. 'No person shall be appointed to the Police Force unless he be of sound constitution, active and able-bodied, able to ride, of good character, able to read and write either the English or French language and between the ages of 18 and 40 years.' This extract had shown Hector that he could easily qualify.

The clipping came from a Toronto paper and was dated August, 1873.

Here was his chance. It was 'now or never.' Fate or Destiny had placed that item in his hands, for a purpose, and that purpose must be fulfilled. Then and there, Hector had resolved to accept the chance....

There was in the dining-room at Silvercrest, carved in stone above the fireplace, a crest and motto, the coat-of-arms of the Colonel's branch of the Adair family. Hector, in the old days, had eagerly gained from his father a full knowledge of the meaning of every device and had even become capable, in time, of reciting every syllable of the heraldic language describing the coat-of-arms. This had been placed upon the shield to commemorate the gallantry of an Adair at Bannockburn; that to symbolize the endurance of another at Sluys. The history of the family was written in the design. And it bore not one vestige of dishonour.

"Remember, Hector," the Colonel had often said fiercely, "the shield is clean. Mind you keep it so!"

Beneath the clean shield was the motto, consisting of two words only, but in these words also might be read the story of a mighty line:

'Strong.—Steadfast.'

All that 'Strong' can mean, all that 'Steadfast' can imply,, the Adairs had always been. Woe betide the luckless wight who should be the first to deviate from it!

'Strong! Steadfast!'

Strong and steadfast Hector would have to be if he was to maintain the honour of the Adairs in the times before him. His feet were on the sunset trail. At its end was Life, swift and fierce and terrible. Years and years of battling through wild winters and blazing summers, on barren mountains, lifeless prairies, and death-dominated rivers lay before him and in that Western land the hands of many men—merciless Indians, murderous horse-thieves, gamblers, whiskey-traders and desperadoes—would be against him—against him and his comrades of the Police. He knew it. He knew that the Force would be but a handful scattered over a vast wilderness which it must protect and eventually free from the domination of innumerable enemies. He knew the greatness of the task to be achieved before the Flag could wave in security from sea to sea. Here was a wonderful opportunity, a real fight to win, a splendid objective. It should have frightened him. Instead he welcomed it. He was as fitted for the work before him as any man could be.

'Strong. Steadfast.'

2

At Winnipeg, straggling its hundred-odd houses, its dozen stores, its sturdy churches and its garish saloons along the muddy trail, the column found the entire population awaiting them. During the winter the Police had made many staunch friends. There were cheery greetings enough and to spare for Hector as he rode along with his comrades through the little crowd. Here was a shout and a wave from Big Jim Hackett, owner of the Hell's Gate saloon, there a smiling blush from pretty Miss Sinclair, one of the local lights, which drew upon him a volley of chaff. Stout, grizzled, jovial and 'unco' canny' Andrew Ferguson, the village baker, received him with a round of Gaelic and a burst of Cree which betrayed his parentage. Johnny Oakdale, the little hardware man with whom Hector had become pleasantly intimate when they erected stoves at the lower fort months before, gave him a shake of the hand which was worth a dozen noisier welcomes.

Now that the hour when he must part with these great-hearted friends was actually upon him, Hector found himself stirred with regret. Recalling happy times, he almost wished that he could remain in the settlement forever or, better still, take the entire population into the North-West with him.

II

Arriving at Dufferin, they joined in preparing for their tremendous march. The Commissioner and the rest of the Force came into camp, bringing more horses and wagons and an army of agricultural implements—they would be dependent entirely on themselves for food in the country to which they were going. A marvellous atmosphere took possession of the camp. The crews of the Golden Hind, the Santa Maria and the Nonsuch, which carried Drake and Columbus and the first officers of the Hudson's Bay Company into the new and unknown world, must have felt just such an atmosphere as they got ready for sea. La Verandrye, Champlain, La Salle were close kin to the men of the Mounted Police assembling at Dufferin.

Languid June drifted into the sunny splendors of July and the white-helmeted, red-coated little column began its march Westward.

To establish posts through that great wilderness, now tenanted only by a few white settlers, Hudson's Bay traders and other traders who dealt in poison-whiskey with nomadic bands of Indians; and from these posts to enforce over every yard of that immensity the laws of Canada—that was their task. They played the dual role of soldier-pioneers.

But they were soldiers and soldiers only in the routine that governed them in camp and on the march. From dawn to dusk, each day slipped easily by. The advance led them over mile on mile of wind-swept prairie blazing with wild flowers, trilling with the songs of birds and insects, dappled with sun and shadow, sweetly perfumed, a hundred tales of hoof and claw on its broad surface and the cloudless sky above. Sunset, when the tired teams halted, the tents sprang up, the wagons marshalled themselves into line abreast, the scouts and guards came loping in and the smoke of cooking fires arose—sunset, when the glories of the Kingdom of

Heaven flamed for a moment in the dusk, was an hour of splendor. Then, after supper, the older officers told them strange stories, they sang choruses to the accompaniment of mouth-organ, concertina or violin, and the happy half-breed drivers danced the Red River jig on a special door they carried in the carts. Coffee followed and a general departure to the tents; more laughing as all hands settled down for the night; and so they came to the last bugle-call of a day punctuated by bugle-calls, 'Lights Out' quivered dolefully through the lines, the orange cones of glowing canvas vanished one by one and the deep silence of night in vast spaces, broken only by the occasional stamping of restless horses, descended on the camp, leaving the sentries to watch the stars alone.

There was plenty of hard work and much discomfort, rising towards the end, for some of them, to real hardship. But they were young and as keen and vigorous as steel blades. They cheerfully stood it all.

Hector preferred duty with the advance-guard or scouts to anything else. There was much more to see and do there, and courage, strength and intense vigilance were essential. Many useful lessons were to be learned in front and, above all, the teacher was the finest scout, the wisest plainsman, the surest horseman in the column, old in Indian fighting, versed in all the legends of the country, knowing the Indians as a mother knows her children and the prairies as a postman knows his beat. Though usually silent and distant, this giant seemed to take a fancy to Hector and unbent to him always. After a time they made a custom of riding together. He was guide and interpreter; a quarter breed; and Martin Brent his name.

Old Martin told Hector everything he knew, and started him fairly off towards being one of the best men in the

Force.

As they moved forward, week by week, through sun and storm, intense heat, dead calm, cold rain and blustering wind, the country changed. The wide levels of plain dotted with small bushes became little ridges, sharp bluffs and rounded hills. Then a maze of rivers appeared before them, running in all directions but Martin led them unerringly through. Next came a bolder roll of prairie, with wider valleys and steeper, larger crests, sweeping on again to blend with the confused jumble of foot-hills which fringe the Rocky Mountains. The Commissioner at last turned back Eastward. The Assistant-Commissioner pushed on, Hector's division with him. Indians hovered restlessly on their flanks and came to visit them with tokens of friendship. Not a shot was fired against them. Once they passed through immense herds of buffalo, covering the plains for miles like a restless sea, the rear-guard of a tribe fast disappearing. At last the long-expected mountains rose in the Assistant-Commissioner's path, marking the limits of their journey, a line of blanketed chiefs, a ridge of wintry sea hurling silvery crests against long palisades of angry sunset.

Here they halted and prepared to build their barracks, the great trek ended.

A thousand miles, or little less, had been covered since they left Dufferin. In their trail blossomed flowers of law and order. The wilderness became a Land of Promise as they passed. Today the iron road, laden with the traffic of a continent, gleams where their wagons rolled. Prosperous farms rise everywhere on the expanse which to them was only an Indian hunting-ground. Young towns stand where they pitched their lonely tents. Proud cities blaze and thunder where they built their lonely forts and in peace and ease a People reap the harvest sown by them in peril and privation.

III

Before winter took full command the barracks were built—rough cabins, enclosed in a stockade—and the Flag hoisted. They christened the place Fort Macleod, in honour of their chief.

In the meantime, callers came and left their cards, came from everywhere—white men and Indians—but especially Indians. One of the first visitors was Crowfoot, chief of the Blackfoot Nation, who rode in with his fellow-chiefs of the Bloods and Piegans, a Prince of the Plains surrounded by his Court. They were tall, straight, fearless men, well armed, dressed in buffalo-robes or gay blankets, richly beaded moccasins and leggings, brass rings round their neat black braids, feathers in their hair. Martin began the pow-wow by presenting them to the Assistant-Commissioner. Then they squatted in a semi-circle before him and passed around the pipe of peace.

When the Colonel had explained the why and wherefore of the Force and Martin had interpreted, his long hair thrown back, his eyes blazing, the chiefs stood up in turn and gave thanks. They told of the devastating fire-water, of women carried away, of robes and horses stolen, of pillage and butchery endured at the hands of beastly white men. They showed themselves facing starvation through the wanton destruction of the buffalo. But now, they said, those days were past.

"Before you came, we crept in terror of our lives," said The Gopher. "Today we walk erect and are men."

Most eloquent of all was Crowfoot himself.

"Hear me," he began, "for I speak for every man, woman and child of the Blackfoot Nation." Then, baring his arm and with proud gestures, he went on. "I thank the Great White Mother and the One Above who rules us all because they have sent to us the Shagalasha, the red-coats, to save us from the bad white man and from ourselves. The Shagalasha are our friends. When we see them we lower our rifles and show them the open hand. What you have said is good and what you say shall be the law. I have spoken."

Hector, hearing these words interpreted, remembered how they had marched unchallenged through thousands of Indians, looked at his scarlet coat and, with a strange thrill of pride, understood.

Other visitors came to Fort Macleod in those early days—white men—spies sent by the whiskey-traders, curious American horsemen, and a few settlers, who thanked God, as Crowfoot had done, for sending the Police to deliver them from the drunken Indian and the low-down white. Of the settlers, none was so thankful, none became so popular in the course of a few calls, as Joe Welland, who lived on a homestead of sorts some sixty miles to the south, on St. Mary's River.

A keen-faced, clean-shaven, strong-handed man was Welland, tawny-haired, lean, sinewy as a broncho and as hard. He came in one day from what he called his 'ranch,' riding a fast mustang which he handled as easily as an expert dancer handles his partner on a ball-room floor. First he called on the Assistant-Commissioner, hat in hand, showing him the respect which was his due and telling him that the arrival of the Police was something for which he had prayed ever since he first came West. Thence he went to see 'the boys,' who received him cordially and consented to smoke some excellent cigars which, somehow, even in that wilderness, he could offer them. He revealed a quiet, congenial manner and wits which were as sharp as needles.

His antecedents, such as they were, were satisfactory, representing all his respectable neighbours knew of him, which was not much. From them the boys learned: First, that Welland was well educated; second, had been born in North America, none knew exactly where; third, had lived in the country at least ten years; fourth, was of unimpeachable character; fifth, seemed apparently well off; sixth, was one of the 'livest' men in the Canadian North-West; seventh, like most of his fellows, was a squaw-man.

"You'll like Welland," said the honest traders. "He's dead against the whiskey-men. And he'll surely help to make things lively!"

IV

A short time before Christmas Welland met and halted Hector on the trail outside the fort.

"We're going to have as real a Christmas here as you can get in this God-forsaken country, Hector," he announced. "The officers and men will chip in a day's pay. The store-keepers will help us out and we'll form a citizens' committee. We're going to have a dance and dinner and ask every decent man and woman we can lay our hands on. The Old Man's consented, but it's a secret so far. So mum's the word."

"That's fine, Joe," said Hector—there had grown up quite an intimacy between them. "Who started the idea? First I've heard of it."

"S-s-h!" replied Welland, twinkling. "Not a word, boy. I—I started it myself. You see, I thought this-ud be a lonely Christmas for you young fellows, the first in a strange land, and we'd better help to make it a merry one. A sort of combined affair, it'll be, d'you see—welcome on our part, house-warming on yours."

"Good of you, Joe," Hector asserted.

"Bosh! Another thing—I'm going to suggest you for your committee."

"Oh, no!" exclaimed Hector. "Don't do that, Joe."

"Why not?" asked Welland, smiling a little.

"Well—you see—first of all—I—the boys might think I'd put you up to it. They know we're friendly. Second, I don't want to push myself. If they want to elect me, let them do it on their own. Besides, I don't know anything about these things."

Welland set out to crush this youthful modesty.

"Now, look, Hec'. This will be done quiet and nice and proper. There won't be any harming you in the eyes of the boys. I'll just tip Sergeant-Major Whittaker that I want you on the committee because I think you're one of the most suitable men they can elect. He'll put you forward—he thinks as I do—and then you'll get a place. You're a gentleman born. You've seen how parties should be run—yes, you have!—and you're popular. Young? Hang it, boy! What does your age matter? There's not a more manly or popular character in the whole Force. Come, Hec', to oblige me! Well, I don't care whether you like it or not—you're going on this committee!"

With that he rode away.

Hector hated this favouritism but was none the less flattered. Welland, it seemed, had taken a fancy to him at the first meeting—had apparently singled him out from the ruck. And now this remarkable demonstration of the man's esteem had come. Welland was one of the best friends of the Force in the country. To be singled out for his favours was a high compliment. But Hector didn't want to be on the committee!

A few days later, at Sergeant-Major Whittaker's instigation, he found himself elected. Preparations commenced. Welland was mainly responsible for their success.

Welland it was who acted as the link between the Police and the civilians, advised the Assistant-Commissioner on a hundred points and, though he modestly refused a place on the committee himself, did more than any other man to help the thing forward. He won the co-operation of the grouchiest store-keepers; solved the difficulty of obtaining enough flags to decorate the ball-room by having them manufactured at Fort Benton, in Montana, the nearest town; soothed all disunity among the members of the citizens' committee with a quiet word here, a story there; and oiled all the wheels of the preliminaries with a master-hand.

And, when the festivities had actually started, Welland was always at hand. If a guest became unruly, he brought him to his senses without disturbing for one moment the smooth tide of convivial joy. If the fiddlers got drunk before the dance, Welland had them in their places, tuning up, as fresh as daisies, when the hour for music came. To crown it all, he was so self-effacing that he might have been a helpful unseen spirit rather than a man.

As for Hector, the Colonel afterwards congratulated him on the part he had played in the arrangements.

"I owe this to Welland," Hector thought, a sentiment which would have greatly pleased that honest gentleman, as it happened to be true.

3

But there was more work than play for the Police in those early days, when they were striking at the roots of disorder.

The most powerful of their foes was the whiskey-trader. To the extermination of the whiskey-trader they directed a special campaign. Hardly a day went by through all the winter which did not see an expedition starting out to raid some distant outfit or returning with prisoners and spoil. A long ride through solitary darkness, a careful bit of scouting to surround the blissfully ignorant camp, a sudden swoop at dawn with levelled carbines and sometimes with a flurry of resistance; the guilty parties taken, the robes and liquor confiscated—thus went the programme. Courage, endurance, cunning, endless patience were all required to win success in the great game and no man employed on a whiskey raid could claim that his talents were wasted.

'Red-hot' Dan was operator, single-handed, of a den near the boundary-line. He was also a desperate character.

But no law-breaker, however desperate, could go unchallenged now. The Police must deal with him as with all. An exception, however, was made to this extent: the party was picked unusually carefully.

Sergeant-Major Whittaker led it. Martin Brent went with him as scout and guide. The three others were Constable Cranbrook; Constable Bland, the finest marksman in the Force; and Constable Adair.

The trumpeter was sounding 'Reveille' as they left Fort Macleod and turned their horses southward.

At dusk they reached Joe Welland's shack, where they proposed to pass the night. A light gleamed through the grimy panes.

"The King's in his Castle," remarked Cranbrook.

Sergeant-Major Whittaker knocked. Welland opened the door, a startled exclamation springing to his lips at sight of the scarlet coats.

"Good God!" he cried sharply. Then, "Oh, it's you! You scared me, boys. I never know who's prowling 'round in parts like these. But welcome—come right in."

"Did you think we'd come for you, old chap?" laughed Cranbrook, as they clanked across the threshold.

"You might have done, at that!" Welland grinned. "But what's the game, boys? Eh? Never mind that now, though. Whatever it is, you'll eat and spend the night here. I won't take 'No.'"

"Here's our orders to you, Welland," replied the Sergeant-Major. "A place for five horses; water for the same; use of your fire for cooking grub for four hungry men and a boy"—with a smiling nod at Hector—"and shelter till we choose to move."

"Done! I know you're after some darn whiskey-trader; so you're welcome more than ever," cried Welland. "Hey, Lizzie; fix fire, get table ready—quick, mighty quick. You're going to eat on me, Sergeant-Major."

At Welland's command, his squaw, a poor, bedraggled object, in home-made skirt and blanket, her hair braided and looped up behind, emerged from a corner and began to obey the orders of her lord and master.

"Now, the stable. Not a soul will guess your horses are there!"

He was a shrewd customer.

The horses put up, they all sat down to supper, while Lizzie waited on them. Welland treated her roughly and Hector's estimation of him bumped down suddenly. As they ate, Hector studied the room, which he had never seen before. It gave a not unfavourable insight into the owner's character. Surprisingly well furnished, it was carpeted in buffalo robes, its walls were hung with wolf skins, and pictures of places and people dear to Welland alternated with cuts from magazines to give it a touch of civilization. A couch covered by a gay Navajo blanket occupied a corner. Several first-class rifles stood in racks. There were books on shelves. This was the home of a man of at least some culture.

"Think it funny to see those bindings here, Hec'?" the observant Welland asked. "I tell you, Joe's not as rough a diamond as he looks. I couldn't leave Bill Shakespeare behind me when I first came West; and I find a lot of people in these parts remind me of Don Quixote!"

Hector wondered if that was a dig at the Police. But he let it pass.

After supper, Welland for the first time broached the subject of their expedition.

"You'll find that 'Red-hot' Dan a real tough nut to crack," he said.

Hector wondered how Welland had guessed. Trained by this time to conceal his thoughts, however, he gave no sign. The laconic Martin did not move a muscle. The road was clear for Sergeant-Major Whittaker.

"I've heard he is," he answered smoothly. No blind betrayal of their purpose there!

"You have? Then you'll be careful what you do."

"When we arrest him—yes."

"I'd shoot at sight if I were you."

"We never shoot at sight in the Police, Joe."

"But 'Red-hot' Dan does."

"What's he got to do with us?"

"See here, Sergeant-Major—why not trust me? You needn't play you're not going after Dan, because I know you are. He's the only whiskey-trader operating 'round here and——"

"Trust you? Why, of course we trust you!" laughed the cunning Sergeant-Major. "But we don't talk about our work to—outsiders."

"I guess I should be snubbed!" said Welland. "That's a nasty slap to a man who wants to help you. I'm talking for your good when I tell you Dan's a devil. Wait till I tell you——"

And he narrated several stories of the trader's daring.

"Now," he concluded, "if that won't satisfy you, ask Martin there. Isn't Dan a dangerous man, Martin?"

Martin, apparently asleep, pricked up his ears like a dozing dog.

"You bet," he said.

"There!" Welland declared. "The whole country knows these things. You're new—and you should be warned."

"Trying to frighten us?" the Sergeant-Major asked.

"Yes, I am. If you'll take my tip, you'll go back to Fort Macleod for reinforcements. Five of you can't take Dan without bloodshed."

"You don't think much of us, that's sure." Whittaker smiled. "Now look, Joe Welland! We appreciate your warnings—but—how d'you know we're after 'Red-hot' Dan? And suppose we were—could we go back to the fort without trying to get him? How about Dan? Wouldn't he get wind of us and skip while we were away? How about our orders? But what's the use? Who said we're after him?"

"You're taking chances!"

"We can take 'em!" said the Sergeant-Major, fiercely brushing his moustaches.

"All right. Have it your own way! I've warned you, anyhow." Welland was obviously disappointed. "My hands are clean!"

At four o'clock, having covered the twenty miles between Welland's and the trader's in excellent time, they found themselves near the scene of action. The Sergeant-Major ordered Cranbrook to stay behind with the horses and the rest of them crawled to the edge of the ridge overlooking 'Red-hot' Dan's cabin.

Hector's heart beat fast. This was the first experience promising real danger which had fallen to him since he joined the Force.

Down in the long valley they saw the hut—grey, lonely, forbidding, in the dawn. But—unexpected blow!—it seemed deserted. In all the valley there was no sign of life. The shack was like a skull in the desert. Life had been there. It was there no longer. Had the wolf scented their coming and—taken to his heels?

"By the Lord!" muttered the Sergeant-Major, between clenched teeth, "the beggar's gone!"

Martin smiled cunningly.

"You think so? I don't! You see no trail going away—no. The beggar home, all right! But he play dead. No time get away, so he think: 'Pretend me gone. Foolum.' See?"

Light dawned on the Sergeant-Major's countenance.

"Now, listen: Dead snake always most bad snake. Always be more careful with dead snake. Make good plan now—he there, I bet you."

And so, assuming Dan at home, they made their plan. Keeping under cover, they crept to a point very near the shack. Sergeant-Major Whittaker posted Bland to cover the door from one hand, Martin from the other. To order the trader to come out was, they knew, quite useless. He would not surrender while the shack afforded him shelter. They must persuade him to admit them—then seize him. At the first sign of resistance, Martin and Bland were to shoot the man dead as he stood in the doorway.

"Come on, Adair," the Sergeant-Major smiled coolly. "You an' me must do the dirty work. Keep the bracelets handy."

So, their revolvers in their holsters, the pair of them approached the shack on the blind or windowless side. The sun was almost over the horizon. No sound, no movement betrayed a human presence in the shack. But one significant fact became obvious as they crept 'round to the front. The windows had been stoutly barricaded.

Close to the door they were, now—the air taut as a violin string.

The Sergeant-Major, motioning to Hector to remain where he was, strode boldly from cover and rapped thunderously on the heavy portal.

They heard only the echoes dapping through the rooms. Was there really no one there?

Again the Sergeant-Major knocked—twice—three times—without result. Then, like a drill instructor on the square, he bellowed:

"Open that door there—in the Queen's name!"

And then the answer came. A streak of flame flashed out, and a deafening report. Hector heard the bullet zip past him. The Sergeant-Major pitched down upon his face.

'Red-hot' Dan was 'Red-hot' Dan indeed—and decidedly at home!

III

Hector acted as his natural courage bade him; but how he got the Sergeant-Major away he never rightly knew. Bullets buzzed all 'round him as Martin and Bland maintained a rapid fire to cover his retreat. Through a tiny loophole in one of the barricaded windows keen eyes watched him as he dropped on his knees and crawled out to the motionless form. From this loophole other bullets came ringing, in quest of his life. Mechanically he lifted the little Sergeant-Major and slung him over his shoulders—his hot young strength standing him in good stead. A minute more and he was safely back with Bland and Martin, gazing stupidly at the Sergeant-Major, now lying on the ground, and asking, "Is he dead?"

His clothes were shot through, his hands bloody and he felt sick and shaken. But the spasm passed, leaving him—ready for anything.

Bred and trained for leadership, this was his opportunity. The Sergeant-Major knocked out, command of the party fell naturally into Hector's hands, hands preordained and long prepared to grapple with just such a menace. He had no thought of the benefits which would come to him if he dealt with it successfully. He only saw that someone must take the Sergeant-Major's place. He felt his powers rising to the occasion like a thoroughbred rising to a leap.

The Sergeant-Major, shot through the chest, was not dead but in great pain. Obviously, he must be sent away at once. Hector, now firmly in the saddle of authority, was already at grips with his problems.

"Tommy," he said to Bland, "I want you to take the Sergeant-Major back to Cranbrook. He'll manage it if you take your time. Then get on your horse, put the S.-M. on his, and ride back to Welland's. After you get there, leave him with Welland and go on to the fort. Report to the Colonel and he'll send a cart and medical help to Welland's. Is that all clear?"

Bland nodded.

"Then listen. When you start for Welland's, ride with the Sergeant-Major over that ridge there, in front of the shack. Tell Cranbrook to follow you, leaving the other horses hobbled for the time being. After you're over that ridge, make straight for Welland's, while Cranbrook will go back by a detour, under cover, to where he leaves the horses and wait till we come. I'll tell you why I want this done. The fellow in that shack only knows that there are three of us—the S.-M. and myself, because he saw us, and someone else who fired at the house while I brought the S.-M. back. So when he sees three of you, one wounded, ride back over that ridge, he'll think you the whole party—that we've all gone off. Then he'll come out or get careless and we can surprise him. Savvy?"

"You're a corker, Hec'!" said Bland.

Hector's instructions were carried out precisely. In half an hour he saw three horsemen move slowly over the ridge, one supported by a rider on each side. They were in full view from the barricaded windows and their scarlet coats could be seen.

But the garrison of the shack was in no hurry to emerge. An hour passed—two—three. Hunger dug its claws into Hector. Nevertheless, he decided to wait till doomsday. Patience, he knew, would decide this battle. The force that held out longest would win.

If only 'Red-hot' Dan and his colleagues—if he had any—would show their noses for just a minute, the whole thing would be over. Hector's game was to hold them up, keeping under cover himself and to shoot them out of hand if they resisted. Dan, however, was too sly a bird. The afternoon wore on and still no sign of him was seen. Either he feared a trap or was perfectly content to spend the day indoors.

It was when his patience was exhausted that Hector evolved his second scheme. Pondering the situation, it came to him in a flash of inspiration. He confided in Martin. The interpreter's patience was inexhaustible and, knowing that the waiting game was the sure game, he had not troubled to seek out any other. But now he vowed that the little tenderfoot was a clever little fellow and threw himself whole-heartedly into the plan.

Hector, taking off his boots, crawled up behind the shack and so to the roof, taking pains to make no noise. Then he awaited developments.

In time another actor came upon the scene, but from the front and marching openly forward. He was a half-naked Indian carrying a rifle in his hand. He knocked at the door. Hector's spirits leaped. The first sound of a human voice from within came floating gruffly upward:

"Who's there?"

The Indian, in Blackfoot, demanded fire-water. A panel in the door was opened and a face looked out cautiously. The moment, now, was at hand. Would the trader open the door?

'Red-hot' Dan, the Police forgotten, emerged, a cupful of liquor in his hand. The Indian raised his eyes—the signal meaning they had only one man to conquer. Straight and true, with deadly force and swiftness, Hector launched himself full upon the trader. The Blackfoot dropped his rifle, too. Their enemy resisted desperately, the atmosphere electric with his fair round oaths. But Hector's weight and strength and Martin's powerful aid—the Blackfoot was only Martin, undressed for the occasion—were far too much for him. In half a minute all was over. Hector had the handcuffs on his victim and 'Red-hot' Dan, terror of the plains, fiercest whiskey-trader in the country, lay sprawling beneath him, a hoodwinked prisoner.

IV

The Assistant-Commissioner promoted Hector to corporal for that day's capture, and set his feet on the long, steep road to victory.

From beneath the skirt of the teepee a young prairie chicken emerged—no ordinary prairie chicken, but an absurd thing dressed in a little pair of trousers and a scrap of scarlet blanket. Hector grinned. The chicken stood irresolute, looking wildly 'round for a favourable avenue of escape. While it hesitated, two small brown hands and arms appeared from under the teepee and frantically searched the air. The chicken danced away. A dishevelled head next wriggled its way into the open air, two bright black eyes flashed a pitiful appeal to Hector, a soft voice cried:

"Oh, pony-soldier, please, pony-soldier—catch my prairie chicken—catch my baby!"

Burly Corporal MacFarlane, Hector's companion in this stroll through the Assiniboine encampment, smiled heavily but made no move. Hector started off in pursuit.

The ground was rough, his boots and spurs were very heavy, the agility of the baby was amazing and the crowded teepees were serious obstacles. Hector dashed 'round and 'round, close behind. He tripped, scraped his hands, stumbled up, heard MacFarlane's encouraging "For'ard on!" made another desperate effort, crashed over a box and emerged from the wreckage triumphant, the baby shrilling in his arms.

"Got him, Mac!" he called. "Now, where's the owner of this independent bird?"

He was at the teepee in a moment, but of the owner nothing could be seen. Two years and more had taught him that most Indian women were intensely shy with white men. He had learnt something of their languages from Martin Brent—the knowledge was useful in his work—and by this time could speak them fairly fluently. The little squaw had been overcome by shyness but was not far away.

He summoned her in her own tongue:

"Here is your prairie chicken, O chieftain's daughter! Come and get your prairie chicken!"

No answer came.

"O chieftain's daughter," he cooed seductively, "do not keep the poor pony-soldier waiting. And your baby!"

The charm brought results in time. Two hands were thrust from the door of the teepee, the fingers stretched to take the bird, but of the lady herself nothing was visible.

Hector was disappointed.

"Why don't you come out?" he coaxed. "Surely you will thank the pony-soldier—the poor pony-soldier who ran so far to bring your baby back?"

She came.

Hector had leisure now to confirm first impressions. She was very pretty, in her Indian way. Her gentle eyes, clear and limpid as a fawn's, glanced shyly upward at his own. Her lips, on which the smiles were trembling, were red petals from the prairie rose. The two thick plaits in which her hair was braided were of that rich blue-black which is the exclusive birthright of Indians and Latins. She wore an elaborately beaded buckskin dress, which truly marked her as the daughter of a chief. The rare beauty of her body, unspoilt by heavy work, the looseness of her dress could not conceal. Hector could not place her age, but she was delightfully young; and that was good enough.

"Take it," he said gravely, handing her the bird.

Taking it, her small fingers mingling with his, she spoke at last, a swift smile bringing light to her face, like a rainbow in sad skies.

"Thank you, pony-soldier, for catching my baby."

Serious, then, both were, till all at once the humour of the situation struck her and her smile flashed back to break in little rills of laughter. She laughed like a child, with her whole body. Hector burst out laughing, too, his spirit echoing back her mood. MacFarlane, behind, growled peevishly. A moment more and her shyness was back again. Her pet on her breast, a final word of thanks on her lips, she vanished, leaving Hector standing there.

"You laugh with my daughter, my son? That is good—for to laugh is to be happy."

Hector turned, surprised.

Before him stood a chief—a minor chief, as chiefs went, but as fine a figure as the plains could boast of, the very soul of chieftainship. He was tall and spare, straight and majestic as a pine, dressed in a barbaric splendor which became him to perfection. But his greatness was written mainly in his face. The wisdom of a hundred medicine men, made rich by long years of life, was in it, with strength, true strength—which is utterly devoid of arrogance or vanity—the calmness of a meditative mind, vast dignity and high authority. And his long white hair and mighty war-bonnet framed it all with glory.

"You laugh with her—is it not so?" he said.

"She has a cheerful heart," Hector answered, finding his voice.

"And you," the chief asserted, "you have one, too. But kind also—few white men would run to catch the pet belonging to a little squaw." He smiled. "You are interested in us? So you walk through the camp to see us?"

"Yes," said Hector.

"That is good, for we are brothers, you and I, though I call you 'son.' You must come and see us when you will. We are—you know it?—of the Assiniboines. My name is Sleeping Thunder, and my daughter's name is Moon-on-the-Water. So you will find us."

Moon-on-the-Water! She was like her name.

"I will come and see you soon, Sleeping Thunder," replied Hector.

As they walked away, MacFarlane threw in a ponderous comment.

"Funny old man! Girl's pretty, though—for an In'jun. You made a hit there, Hec'!"

II

Sleeping Thunder's camp was only one of many gathered together that day in the Fort Macleod country, where the Indians were to meet the Queen's officials to make a treaty. Hector's division was there on escort duty.

The years had brought swift and sweeping changes. To-day Hector was a senior sergeant, though still in the early twenties, knowing his work inside out, intimate with the red men, an expert catcher of criminals and particularly of whiskey-traders, his special game. Honest, hard, dangerous work had put the triple chevrons on his arm. And drawing nearer every day, though still a dreary distance off, the first faint flashes of the higher light he sought were slowly opening before his eyes.

The Police had wrought great things in the few years behind them. The whiskey traffic had been much reduced and the old system of trading posts was gone, entirely and forever. The effect had been to convert the Indian to ways of peace. This in turn had brought the settler in who, up till now, had barely dared to show a timid nose in the country south of the Red Deer. Already the plains were dotted with homesteads, and cattle roamed along the grass lands soon to become tenanted by the immense herds of prosperous ranches. More settlers and more settlers were pouring out from the East. Before they could be accommodated, some title to the lands they wanted must be given them. The red men claimed the whole of the Northwest Territories. They were willing to relinquish them in return for certain privileges. So treaties were made with the great tribes in turn. And now the tribes of the Macleod district had come together to make their treaty too.

III

"You have a love for our ways and an interest in our customs?" asked Sleeping Thunder. "You admired our warriors?"

"Yes," Hector answered.

They were standing with Moon outside the chief's teepee on the last day of the treaty celebrations.

"Would you like to see more of them? You have not really seen us until you have seen the Sun Dance, which we hold each year in the summer."

"I want to see much more," said Hector. The romance of the things he had recently witnessed had fascinated him. "I would like to see the Sun Dance."

"Then hear me. If you do not mind camping with Indians, come to us next year and I will show you. I will teach you all our practices, our stories and legends and more of our language. It is too late this year, but next year—. I will send a messenger to tell you where to come and when. I would like you to come—and so would Moon."

"You would like me to come?" Hector asked, smiling at Moon.

She flashed a demure answer with her eyes.

An attractive little thing, this Indian girl!

"Then I will come," said Hector, seizing the opportunity.

With that promise they parted.

IV

In June of the following year, Hector, in frontier outfit; his uniform laid aside, rode out to meet Sleeping Thunder and to see the Sun Dance.

MacFarlane saw him off at the stables.

"Who is she, Hec'?" he asked, raising his bushy brows and smiling meaningly. "That pretty little squaw, isn't it?"

Hector, whacking the pack-pony into motion and touching up his horse, looked down and smiled in return.

"You will have your little joke, won't you, Mac?" he said. "The girl's got nothing to do with it."

"Hasn't she?" MacFarlane mocked. "Oh, no—not at all!"

On the trail Hector headed southward, thinking of many things.

His interview with Sub-Inspector Lescheneaux, a wizened, bird-like French-Canadian commanding Hector's troop, when asking for leave, had been a droll but pleasing affair, ending very flatteringly.

"No leave ov h'absence since we first cam' out 'ere," the worthy little man had ruminated; "one ov bes' N.C.O.s in dis de-vision, oui; 'as don' more to stamp out d'illicit wheesk-ey traffic den any oder sergeant I know; desires leave ov h'absence for one for'd'night; vraiment, 'e deserve it, too. Eef Inspect-eur Denton 'as no objection, Sergeant, you go by all means. I t'ink, Sergeant-Major Whee-taker, we say dis request granted, eh? Good luck, Sergeant—bon voyage.

Tiens!"

The Sergeant-Major, too, had made Hector happy.

"He's right—right, by God, he is! Since that day at 'Red-hot' Dan's, Adair, yes, and before that, I marked you for a winner. You've certainly earned your little rest—damn my buttons, yes!"

This was true, all of it. Hector had worked hard. He had acquired a reputation in the Force as one of the smartest hunters of whiskey-runners it possessed.

But there were flies in the ointment and snakes in the grass. He had not yet been able, for all his hard work, to put down the traffic in the district allotted to him. Most of the traders and runners had long since fallen into his hands. Yet there was still a great deal of trading the source of which he could not trace. Some underground current was pouring through the district carrying liquor to the Indians. During the past few months he had made a particularly stern effort to dam the flood. Success would temporarily reward him. Then, suddenly, without warning, the stream would bubble out in some new spot—in twenty spots at once. The mystery troubled him. The hold it had secured on him made itself obvious in the fact that, though he had fixedly resolved to forget it for a fortnight, it had him now.

But the glorious appeal of the morning soon drove it from his mind. It was full June, the sky was a light blue dome, golden at bottom, where the sun blazed, and flecked elsewhere with baby clouds drifting before the lazy wind. The long grass, clean, shining, went rippling to the edges of eternity. The larks piped in the hollows and the little gophers sat up to watch him as he passed. Hector was young, the day was young, and troubles fly light as thistledown over the heads of Youth when the time of the year is June.

In a minute or two he was singing a jibing song beloved by the Force, that band of happy warriors who would not take things seriously:

So pass the tea and let us drink
To the guardians of the land.
You bet your life it's not our fault
If whiskey's contraband!

When he sighted Welland's place, where he planned to spend the night, his roving fancy clicked sharply back to roost and turned to Welland.

The friendship between them, though it had prospered in the years now gone, had never reached real intimacy. But Welland's fortunes had been amazingly strengthened during recent times. Prosperity seemed to come to him unsought There was something almost strange in it. Probably he had money invested elsewhere. As men count wealth in other places, he was not yet a Crœsus, of course, but a great improvement was palpably evident. Several new sheds and stables; acres of cultivated ground; cattle and horses; two wagons in the yard; the shack extended and freshly painted—these were obvious additions to the real and personal property owned by Welland when the Police first came to the country. Had he fallen heir to Aladdin's lamp? How, otherwise, had he acquired all this so easily?

As Hector rode slowly down upon the homestead through the velvet dusk, a strange thing happened. From the house he heard an awesome, chilling sound—dull, measured, heavy,—like blows on raw beef. And this sound was punctuated by several low screams, each whimpering, one by one, into a moan. Completely baffled, he dismounted near the stables, raised the 'long yell' that common courtesy demanded, and waited.

Welland came out, peering through the gloom.

"It's me, Joe," Hector called. "Adair!"

"Oh, that you, Hec'?" Welland responded with genuine pleasure. "Good boy! What brings you here this time o' night?"

Hector told him, still wondering——

"Leave, eh? Going down to Milk River, eh? Fine! Fine! Of course you'll spend the night here, and feed, too. Come on! I'll take your horses."

When they entered the house, Lizzie was there, smiling cheerily enough on Hector, whom she knew well by this time—Lizzie, in a new striped skirt, sharing her man's prosperity.

"It couldn't be," Hector decided. Thereupon he placed what he had heard aside, in one of those innumerable pigeonholes of memory, where facts and incidents are unconsciously stowed away till wanted.

In the morning Welland gave him surprise No. 2.

"Hec', you're interested in the suppression of the liquor traffic," he asserted. "I don't know if you've come across this arrangement, though. It's one of the neatest things devised yet."

He handed him that common relic of the prairie, a buffalo skull.

"The horns, as you know, are hollow. The tips have been cleverly cut off and made into caps, to act as corks. You pour in the whiskey and put the caps on. Perfectly tight—perfectly safe! Load a cart up with buffalo skulls, same as all the Indians are doing now, mix a few of these among 'em and you can get your stuff into any reserve in the country without being caught. Who'd suspect a wagonload of buffalo skulls?"

Hector examined it, brain busy.

"Where did you get it?"

"One of those In'juns you arrested about two weeks ago gave it to me. I did him a good turn once. Want it?"

"I might get it when I come back. Here's how!"

"All right. Good hunting!"

Trouble brooded on Hector's face as he turned his horses out into the morning.

He was miles on his way before the holiday spirit came back to him and the buffalo skull went bang into its pigeon-hole.

Milk River, now! And Moon! And Sleeping Thunder!

V

The nights between the days which witnessed the Sun Dance Hector thought wonderful, for it was then that Sleeping Thunder opened his heart. Each night they sat beside the crimson fire, before the teepee, under a splendid canopy of purple strewn with stars. The silence of the plains, with only the howl of a lonely wolf by way of contrast, was about them as they sat, their voices took on mystic qualities unknown to them by day, the air was tense with hidden forces. Nothing stirred and there was nothing to divert them but the flitting form of Moon, attending the fire.

Hector spoke of one thing which dominated his mind, puzzling him.

"At this meeting, Sleeping Thunder, I have seen two ceremonies: one the making of a brave, the other the renewal of the vows of wives and maidens. To me these are as far apart as sun and earth. The first, to me—and I speak for all white men—is barbarous and cruel. But the second is very beautiful. Why do we find these things in the same race and practised by one people?"

Sleeping Thunder, answering him, revealed the entire sum and substance of his Indian philosophy:

"Because you find a thing you think terrible standing side by side with something that is beautiful, you are puzzled. But there is nothing strange in this. It is true to Nature. In one man, to say nothing of peoples, you will find great evils dwelling with much that is good. In the white race, as in the Indian, practices that are beautiful and practices that are ugly walk hand in hand. The white man's law, shielding the weak from the strong, is beautiful. The white man's gambling dens and saloons are not. The Indians, my son, are not the only people possessed at once by good and evil!"

The old man smiled, his bright eyes fixed on Hector.

"But is it evil——" he resumed, "this ceremony of making warriors? What, after all, do we most admire in a man? White men and red alike, we especially admire strength, courage and fortitude. You are content to await the great test of action to prove that your comrades possess these qualities. Till then you credit them with all the strength, courage and fortitude they should rightly have. But we Indians, we are not so easily satisfied. We demand that a young man prove himself before the hour of action. When danger rises in your very path and Death awaits you with his arrow on the string, that is no time, we say, to test a man for the first time. Your safety, perhaps your life, depends, in that moment, on the courage, strength and fortitude of those about you. Then surely you should see that those about you are brave and strong and hardy before entrusting either life or safety to their keeping? That is wisdom, my son, that is right. The boy must show that he is fit to go before we take him with us. Therefore, we try him in the Sun Dance. If he succeeds—then, we need have no further doubts. If he fails—the lives of men are saved and no needless risks are encountered by the remainder of the tribe. The test is severe? Yes; because, otherwise, it would be worthless. But no lasting injury results. What, then, are a few drops of blood, a little agony?

"My son, the Indian does not shun, he embraces the opportunity of that ceremony. Does it not show that he has courage, strength and fortitude, which crown a man with glory as his antlers crown the caribou?

"Now in a woman—what do we admire?" The chief's voice grew tender. "Is it gentleness, is it obedience? These things we honour, yes. But greater than these, and higher than them all, is Purity! White men and red alike, that is the thing we would have especially in woman. We are ourselves weak and corrupt. We feel in our hearts the need of something to help us to be better. So we ask that help from these, our women. We make of Purity a torch of light and put that torch in the hands of those we love, to guide us through the storm. We would have our women—" here he swept a hand towards the skies—"as high above us, as white and clear as yonder stars, to show the way, as they do. We would have them like the peaks of the World's Backbone, which you call the Rocky Mountains, looking always, like them, upon our deeds, landmarks, like them, to guide us by day, as the stars guide us by night, crowned with that virtue, Purity, as the peaks are crowned with spotless snow and, like those peaks, so glorious, so unchanging, so near the Great Spirit—nearer, far, than we!—that only to look on them fills our hearts with awe and wonder. So we would have our women.

"But here again the white and red man part. Your women shrink from a public declaration such as ours endure. Unlike you, we do more than teach our women purity. We ask them to dedicate themselves to purity before the eyes of all. We hold that virtue up before them as a thing to be prized. Then is the shame which follows any falling from the heights made trebly terrible. So do our women learn that it is for them to be true to the laws of the Great Spirit and leave love-making to the male—as with birds, animals, fishes, so must it be with men and women."

Moon, in the shadows, stirred restlessly.

"Both these ceremonies, my son, are beautiful, for they glorify strength, courage and fortitude in men, purity in women. Then there is nothing strange in the observance of these ceremonies by one and the same people. I wonder—do you understand now?"

"I think—I think I see," said Hector.

He looked for Moon; but she had disappeared.

VI

When the great meeting was over, Hector said goodbye to Sleeping Thunder.

"You go from us, my son," the old man exclaimed, extending his hand, "knowing far more of my people than when you came. The Indian's ways and the white man's ways are not the same and it is not good that one should take to himself the habits of the other. The Great Spirit made us different and so we should remain. For one, vast cities, such as you have pictured to me—buildings of stone—sheltered lives; for the other, open plains—teepees—and roving lives that are wild and free. But it is good that we should know one another, since, though you are white and we are red, we are not less brothers. For this, at least, you will not regret your visit, O my son, and I will always hold you as a friend—in time of need, especially, a friend. And now you ride back to your people and no-one knows when we will meet again. But we shall meet again, be sure of that!"

Hector smiled.

"I hope so, Sleeping Thunder," he said; then added regretfully, "Tell Moon I am troubled that she was not here to say goodbye. Tell her I do not understand."

Pain momentarily darkened the chief's face. Then he also smiled.

"Who shall read the mind of a woman?" he questioned. "Go your way. I will tell her."

Again they shook hands. Hector wheeled his horses and rode away.

An Indian watched his going from a clump of bushes on the outskirts of the camp, satisfaction gleaming in his eyes.

From the shadows, night after night, he had sullenly watched the stranger talking with the chief outside the teepee, watched him sitting with the father of Moon.

Loud Gun was glad to see the last of the white man.

5

The country round Fort Walsh lay deep in snow. The cold was intense. Darkness was falling.

Hector, turning back to the stove from this cheerless prospect, thanked God that no law-breaker—no whiskey-runner especially—was likely to be out on such a day, and hence, that he himself was unlikely to be required to take the trail.

He looked at the thermometer hanging in the window.

"Thirty below!" he said to himself. "I pity the poor Nitchies in their teepees."

The poor Indians well merited a little pity. This was, for them, a small-pox winter, a famine winter. Throughout the district, they were dying by thousands. The Mounted Police were working hard to save them, issuing rations and ammunition to the bands that crowded to them for aid. There were men out on the job at that moment. But they could do very little among so many.

Hector, dozing by the fire, thought suddenly of Moon and Sleeping Thunder, contrasting the terrible situation of to-day with that seen in the happy camp at Milk River months before. He wondered if any harm had come to them.

The door swung open to admit MacFarlane.

"Come in, Mac," Hector welcomed him. "Guard mounted?"

"Yes," said MacFarlane.

He plumped down in his ponderous way upon his comrade's cot.

"There's an In'jun outside, Hec'—wants to see you."

"An Indian?"

"Yes. Funniest thing," he chuckled. "Won't see anyone else. 'Sergeant Adair'—those were exactly the words. The nerve of these confounded In'juns! What d'you think? There's the small-pox in camp and they want you there, to save someone or other. As if your life didn't count a damn! I'd have thrown the creature out, but she's so thin and drawn and came so far. You'll have to go and say 'No' yourself," he roared again, slapping his big thigh. "That comes o' making yourself too nice to 'em, Hec'! That comes of your trip to Milk River!"

"Eh?"

Hector had risen. His face reflected none of his comrade's mirth.

"Why, didn't I say? It's that little squaw, Hec'——"

"Where did you leave her?"

"Why, she's out in the yard, Hec'!"—MacFarlane's jaw had dropped. "You're—you're not—going?"

"You fool," Hector flashed. "Certainly I'm going!"

In the yard he found her—haggard, worn out, snow-encrusted, terrible.

"Moon!" he gasped, pity and horror in his voice.

"My father—" she answered dully. "He is dying."

Pleading desperately, trembling hands outstretched, she told him everything. The plague had suddenly appeared on the reserve some weeks before. Sleeping Thunder, to escape it, had taken to wandering with his band in the loneliness of the prairie; but without success. Two—three—had died. Then the chief himself had been stricken. Fear conquered loyalty, and the braves, closing their ears to the prayers of the old man and his daughter, left them to die.

"And Loud Gun?" asked Hector.

She smiled wanly.

"He was kicked by a horse long before. He was in the care of the white doctors—is still there. We were alone."

In this extremity, Sleeping Thunder had thought of Hector. By gigantic efforts Moon had grappled with the difficulties surrounding her and fought a way to Fort Macleod, her father helpless in the sledge behind her.

"We believed you were there," she explained simply.

Despair had almost mastered her when she learned that Hector and his division had been transferred to Fort Walsh. But she had bravely turned her face to the new trail. That morning she had reached a spot some miles distant, pitched camp, made her father as comfortable as possible and pressed on to reach Fort Walsh before dark.

"I know that you will come," she ended.

For a moment he marvelled at the girl's strength and resolution.

Then he voiced another thought.

"But why did you come to me? You might have gone to your Indian agent—to any detachment. At Fort Macleod they would have helped you. Did you try them?"

"No," she said. "We wanted you. You! You alone can save him. We know you will give us what he needs. At Fort Macleod, they would not have helped us as you will help us."

"They would certainly have done so. I can do nothing more than they."

"You can save my father!" she repeated. "Say you will come!"

Hector tried to grasp the beauty and wonder of this thing. He had heard and seen a little of Indian fidelity and trust but until now had never guessed the depths they could fathom. Moon, travelling through all the difficulties confronting her, ignoring every hand that might have helped her, had come to lay her plea before him, with absolute faith that he alone could save her father. The thought humbled him.

But had she thought of the risks he must undergo? She was asking him to face almost certain death, at a time when her own people had deserted her, on the slight justification of their friendship. It was plain that she had thought of all this and in spite of them had not hesitated.

"I will always hold you as a friend—in time of need, especially, a friend."

There, in Sleeping Thunder's words, was the whole substance of the matter.

This was a time of need.

Hector did not waste an instant in considering the risks. He accepted them, in the spirit in which soldiers accept the perils of battle, as inevitable.

"These people—God knows why—" he thought, "rely on me more than on anyone else in the world."

"I will come—at once," he said.

Moon dropped on her knees at his feet and burst into tears.

II

On a fine spring evening, Sleeping Thunder sat with Hector outside the teepee.

The chief, by this time, was fully restored to health.

"In a few days," he said wistfully, "I return to the reserve. The agent has sent for me."

"You should never have left it," Hector reproved him. "You know the law."

"Did the law save me and mine?" the old chief countered. "It could not have done for me what you have done."

Hector smiled quietly. He had given up trying to disillusion the Indian.

"And that," Sleeping Thunder resumed, "brings me to what I wish to say. Have patience. I am old and it is not easy for me to put my thoughts into words."

He gazed steadily out towards the West. The sun was sinking in as perfect a spring sky as Hector had ever seen. The wind rustled the long grass. A bird piped drowsily. A tethered horse stamped. All else was silence.

The figure of Moon, busy round the cooking fire, stood black against the sunset.

"My son, you may remember, long ago, when we were at the Sun Dance camp, I told you that the white man's ways are not our ways and one should not adopt the habits of the other."

"I remember," Hector answered.

"I have changed my mind. That is, I think sometimes the law may be set aside. I wish to set it aside now—today—or soon."

"Go on," said Hector.

"You saved my life. I owe it to you; I know it. No man can owe to another man anything more precious. Then how can he repay such a debt? In this manner only, my son—by offering him the thing he values most in all the world—values as highly as—perhaps more highly than—his life, by tendering it as a gift. So shall he repay the debt he owes."

Hector waited, wondering. The old man sat for a long while silent, his face very tender.

"You see my daughter there—Moon-on-the-Water? Is she not beautiful? She has the eyes of a young deer, her hair is like the sky at midnight, her form like a willow drooping by the river and, when she laughs, we hear the voices of the prairie winds. She is the daughter of a line of mighty warriors and the blood of many chiefs is in her veins. She loves me with all her heart—has she not proved it?—and I know that she would gladly die for me. She is a light among all women. Where will you find her like?"

Hector, remembering her mellow voice, the mystery of her smile, the graceful swaying of her dress, answered,

"Yes, she is beautiful. She loves you."

"She loves me—yes. And I?" The old chief's voice trembled. Far off, through the stillness, faint and doleful, they heard the sound of a trumpet at Fort Walsh. "And I?—I hold her dearer than anything I possess. Many have wooed her, my son, and I have been offered much for her. Ten ponies, fifty rifles, have been offered me by more than one lover. She is worth twenty ponies—compared with other women! And so—you see how dear she is to me and how high the value young men have set upon her."

"Yes," said Hector.

"Then, to repay the debt I owe you with that which is most precious to my heart, I offer you my daughter Moon, to be your wife."

"Your daughter Moon?"

"Yes."

Sleeping Thunder glanced keenly at Hector. The white man was silent; and he could not understand it.

"I know that I am pledging much. It is a great honour I do you, my son." Smiling, the chief stretched out a kindly hand and patted Hector's shoulder. "But of all the world there is no man to whom I would more gladly give my daughter. You are a good man—strong, just, brave, true-hearted. And the debt I owe is great. Be not afraid."

The sunset glow was melting rapidly into the mauves and blues of night. Moon had stopped her work and Hector saw her gazing enraptured towards the West. The light was on her face and, in that moment, she was very beautiful.

But an agony of pity and despair possessed him.

"Sleeping Thunder," he said at last, scarcely knowing what he said, "I know how you have honoured me. Beautiful though your daughter is, faithful and precious to you, you are wrong, my friend—yes, I say it—you do not owe your life to me. The Great Spirit is my witness I speak truth. No, do not disagree with me. My comrade, Murray, he who nursed you through the winter—saved you, not I. This gratitude is lavished over nothing. I value it more than I can say, but still I know it is so."

Struggling with his thoughts, he steeled himself to go on.

"I cannot take this gift, Sleeping Thunder. I have not earned the right. I honour Moon, but—but—there is no love between us—not the love there should be between man and wife."

The old chief flinched and his grey head sank on his breast.

"Then how could good come of such a union? We do not love; and even if we did, your words were truth, Sleeping Thunder. The red man's ways are not our ways. How could she be happy in our life, among our people?"

"There are squaw men among you."

Hector had foreseen the interruption.

"Yes, but do they treat their wives as they should? You know they do not. They make slaves of them and when they are tired or they fall in love with a white woman, they cast them off. I could not do that and would not. But, aside from this, the girl would not be happy. My people—they would look on her with contempt. And as the years went by and cities came where the prairies are desolate today, life would become intolerable for her. You know that is true."

The chief's head had fallen lower still.

"It is true," he whispered.

"I would give my right hand rather than that this should have happened. It cannot be—you know it, Sleeping Thunder."

The old man raised his head suddenly and looked up at the towering young form. He smiled sadly.

"It is true," he answered. "I will say no more."

The night swallowed them.

III

Returning to Fort Walsh, Hector had time to grasp the full significance of the chief's proposal. He had not even faintly foreseen that the old man's gratitude would express itself in the form it had actually taken. Marriage was far from his thoughts. Moon? He was fond of Moon and admired her in many ways—but not in that way. He admired and loved Sleeping Thunder. Hitherto relations between them had been ideal. But this sudden rock had split them and emphasized the unalterable differences in race and life. He wished with all his soul that things could have remained as they were.

Well, the thing was done and over! Only one course of action now remained for either party—to forget it all as soon as possible.

But here he found himself mistaken.

He had just come off duty on the afternoon when Sleeping Thunder was to start for the reserve when he was informed that an Indian was asking for him at the entrance to the fort.

The Indian was Loud Gun, recently back from hospital.

"How!" said Loud Gun, raising a hand in salute and looking down on Hector with his keen, proud eyes.

"How!" returned Hector. "What do you want?"

In a few words, the Indian explained. Moon-on-the-Water Water had sent him. Would Hector go with him and ask no questions?

A few minutes later Hector was in the saddle.

In a little coulee some distance short of Sleeping Thunder's camp, they came suddenly upon Moon.

She was alone. In her richest dress, she made a striking picture—the picture of an ideal Indian princess—calm, strong, beautiful. They greeted her solemnly. As Hector dismounted, she turned to Loud Gun.

"Go over the ridge there," she said, "and wait till I come."

The tone was pitilessly cold. Loud Gun bowed his head submissively and departed without a word.

They were alone, the Indian woman and the white man, face to face.

Moon began.

"You wonder why I sent for you? Perhaps you think I step beyond the rights of squaws?"

Something of her dignity was gone. She smiled wistfully.

"I do wonder why you sent for me, Moon," responded Hector. "But that is all."

There was an awkward pause.

"What is it?" Hector prompted. "Come, what is it, Moon?"

She seemed dumb for a moment. Her head was turned away and her face hidden.

"Is it about your father?"

"Yes," she answered swiftly, with a sudden straightening of her head. "It is about my father—my father—and—"

"Nothing has happened?"

"No. But this matter—I was saying—it is about my father—and—and you—and me!"

He waited. She made a strange, gasping sound in her throat. He began to see a light.

"Moon!" he exclaimed, alarmed.

Her voice came thickly to him.

"My father said he did it as an act of gratitude. You said—you said there was no love between us. He did not do it as an act of gratitude. He did it—" She dropped her bands suddenly and all her strength came to sustain her in that crisis. Her eyes were fearless. "He did it—because I wanted him to do it. You say there is no love between us." Her voice was half a laugh, half a moan. "No love with you, perhaps—but love—great love for you—there is with we!"

"No, Moon, no!"

"Yes!"—a whisper now—a sob that choked her—"I love you, pony-soldier! Pity me! Pity me!"

Amazement, deep concern, an overwhelming grief, swept over Hector. Why had she sent for him for this?

His talk with Sleeping Thunder had been nothing beside the possibilities before him now.

"Moon—"—he fought for words—was the soul of gentleness—"You are not yourself. This cannot be."

She wheeled suddenly, half turning her back. He saw her struggling fiercely with an emotion far more powerful than he had thought could move an Indian woman, least of all Moon.

"I know! I know!" she began. Bitterness, an agony of injured pride, a would-be scornful disregard of the humiliation she was facing, blended in the words that tumbled from her lips. "I know! I know that I—a chief's daughter—am not good enough for you. I know my love would bring you to contempt, would be a drag upon the wheels that take you on to greatness! I know that I would be a jest—a thing to scorn—a—a—"

"Moon," said Hector hotly, "that is not true! Why do you speak so of me?"

She calmed herself with an effort.

"It is not of you I speak," she smiled, with a glance towards him. "You are too kind, too generous for that. You would not scorn me, think that I dishonoured you, consider me a hindrance—no!" Her burning passion mastered her again. "But all your world—the white man's world—would do so. I am the daughter of a chief—I have said it—I am as good, in the eyes of the Great Spirit, as they are. I would be faithful to you and steadfast! I would work for you while life remained in me. But they would spit and laugh at me and call you 'fool' because you married me! Your white world—your white men—ah, and your white! women, your white women!—they would do that. And why? Why?" She rocked in anguish. "Just because I am an Indian—an Indian!"

He could not answer her.

She turned again towards him, terribly overwrought, clutching her breast.

"That is true! You know it!"

"Moon—please do not say these things."

"It is true—will you not admit it? Ah, you will not speak—that means you agree. Because you do not wish to hurt me, you will not speak—but you answer with your silence."

A long pause came. Hector wheeled and looked, unseeing, towards Fort Walsh. Waiting, he heard her fighting back to calmness. She brought herself at last to look at him. His cap was off, his profile cleanly cut against the strong sunlight, his hair ruffled by the soft wind and his scarlet tunic was like a flame to her senses. Her love for him welled up like a strong, deep tide in her desolate heart, mastering her.

"Yet I must face the degradation," she said suddenly, vast tenderness giving a pleading beauty to her voice, "because I love you—I cannot help myself. If I might be your wife—Oh, then I would laugh at all the cruel contempt that poor Indians like me have ever known! But if that cannot be—then let me be your servant and slave. Only to see you, to give my life to your service!"

"Moon," he declared, "I will hear no more. I will not have you speak like this to me!"

"Oh, do not think to save me from shame." She laughed bitterly. "Already I—the daughter of a chief—have broken the laws of my people in telling you my love. I will be an outcast. The sin is on my head. Then let me speak and beg that I may be your slave. I could keep silent no longer. Long have I loved you. You would not hear my father. But I cannot bear to give you up. So I sent for you. And all I ask from you is pity—pity! As for the scorn of my people and yours—I do not care!"

Her passion died away, exhausted, in a little while. And he took her hand and answered her.

"Listen, Moon," he said. "No-one will ever know that this has passed between us. There is no shame in this for you. I hold you too highly ever to grant this prayer of yours. It is not right. Your father said that white men and red cannot live together as man and wife in happiness. There are many Indian warriors, good men, brave and true, who love you. There is Loud Gun—"

"I do not love him!" she flashed.

"There is Loud Gun," he repeated remorselessly. "He loves you. Marry him—and forget me. I will always be your friend, Moon—"

"I cannot forget you. I love you," she persisted.

He shook his head.

"You must. Be sure, you will be happy with him. We must not meet again."

"Pity me!" she whispered.

He turned blindly and heedlessly to his horse.

"Pity me!" she almost shrieked.

But he was mounted now. And, as she flung out a desperate hand, he touched his horse with the spur.

He heard her wailing, Indian fashion, behind him—forced his mount to a fast gallop—faster, faster, to drown that dreadful sound in the rush of wind.

Weak tears blinded him.

So he left her.

IV

Before another day had passed over Fort Walsh, Hector had pondered the situation regarding Moon and come to certain conclusions. First of all, he must obviously see no more of the girl. Secondly, he must do something to repair the damage he had innocently caused. Here he ran into a stone wall. How was he to influence Moon without seeing her himself? In whom could he confide his difficulties, knowing that they would meet with sympathy? Was there anyone he knew with the necessary authority among the Indians, whose words carried weight and whom they loved and trusted?

A battering-ram appeared suddenly from nowhere and smashed the barrier down.

His man was Father Duval.

Father Duval and his work were equally well known to every man in the Police or out. None could say how long he had been in the North-West but only that he seemed as much a part of the country, as strong and staunch and vital and even as eternal as the Rockies. He had made one at the first Christmas celebration of the Force at Fort Macleod six years before and at that time was alleged to have already passed the greater part of his life as a missionary among the tribes in the district. His influence with the Indians, converts and otherwise, was illimitable. They regarded him as their spiritual and temporal parent and went to him for counsel in every predicament. His face was as familiar to them as those of their greatest chiefs, his black-robed figure as common to their camps as a travois or a teepee. The Police recognized him as a useful medium for dealing with the Indians in matters requiring great diplomacy. He was the cheerful, tireless go-between for white man and red, the friend of every Indian, settler and Mounted Policeman.

Father Duval was obviously the man.

As soon as Hector could get away he sought the priest out, riding over to the mission.

"Yes, he will see you," said the lay-brother, lifting a cloud from Hector's heart.

At a knock, the door of the severe little room which was the priest's sanctum was opened and the renowned Father Duval himself stood on the threshold, the kindliest and most lovable of men, his hand outstretched, a twinkling smile upon his rugged face.

"Ah! Entrez, mon petit!" he exclaimed. "Parlez-vous francais?"

Hector shook his head and faltered out a negative. Father Duval's smile deepened and he shrugged his shoulders whimsically.

"Too bad, too bad! Teach yourself, mon petit. It ees ver' important to comprehen' many lan-gwidges, oui. Eh bien! We try to—'ow ees it?—get along without it. Entrez, cher ami, entrez!"

By this time they had shaken hands. Hector jingled into the room, his uniform sounding a note of war in that haunt of peace. The contrast between them was very marked. The older man was like an old tower, strong in age, solid, the younger like a steel blade, keen, vivid, highly tempered. They sat down.

Hector slowly, hesitatingly, began his story. Father Duval listened, one hand on his chin, the other in his sash, his eyes, possessed by just a shadow of encouragement, incessantly fixed on Hector.

When at last Hector ceased, the priest put out a hand and laid it over his, smiling so sympathetically that Hector knew him a friend and helper from that moment.

"You—are you of our faith?" he asked.

Hector shook his head.

"Mon enfant,"—his face seemed to light up with a holy radiance—"it does not matter. I bless you all de same. You 'ave don' right to come to me, Sergeant. All you 'ave don' in dis affaire 'as been right. You 'ave acted as a man ov honour, oui, an' wit' such a beeg, beeg 'art. Ah, mon petit, le Bon Dieu, 'e smile, vraiment, when 'e look down on men lak' you. Mes pauvres petits, de Indian, dey do not get ver' much de consideration you 'ave give to dat ol' chief an' 'is leetle girl. Maintenant, regardez! 'Elp you—but of course—naturelment! Attendee une minute! I 'elp you, oui. For I am well acquaint' wit' dat leetle Moon an' mon brave Sleeping Thunder. Only, 'ow? 'Ow? What to do? Attendez! Attendez!"

Hector waited.

"You say de name ov dat yo'ng fellow, it is—?" the priest queried suddenly.

"Loud Gun," said Hector.

"Loud Gun? Oui. Bon! I 'ave it now. I feex it all. Regardez, mon petit. Don't you worry no more. I will see dat poor leetle girl made 'appy, oui. She marry some good Indian fellow—Loud Gun perhaps, perhaps some oder—but she will forget you an' she will be 'appy, oui, vraiment, I will send you a leetle letter later on an' tell you all about it. An' now, don' you be sad, leetle boy." He patted Hector on the shoulder and beamed up into his eyes with beautiful benevolence. "So de poor Moon, she fall in lov' wit' you, eh?" he added softly. "Vraiment, Sergeant, I am not sooprise'! A fine beeg fellow—an' ver' 'an'some, oui. Now, go—allez, won petit! Forget all dis—an' I write to you. It all come out right soon—you see!"

"God bless you, father!" Hector exclaimed.

His spirits had leaped as high as heaven.

V

"Here's a letter, Hec'," said MacFarlane, three months later. "An In'jun brought it. You're a devil for the In'juns, Hec', old boy!"

Hector took the letter curiously. No Indians were in his mind.

The letter was from Father Duval. Some English lay-brother had written it but the priest's unmistakable signature brought it to a close.

'Dear Sergeant Adair:

Don't fear. She is happy. I have married her myself, today, at my mission here, to Loud Gun. I promise you, her heart is mended! She is happy.

I am always your friend,

FRANCOIS M. DUVAL, O.M.I.'

Slowly Hector read the letter, as slowly tore it into little pieces—as one who tears something that is past and done with—and, going to the open window, let the pieces fly from his fingers in the prairie breeze....

"You're a devil for th' In'juns, Hec'," MacFarlane repeated.

The sweet face of Moon drifted momentarily before Hector's eyes, in the wake of the scraps of paper—fading, at last, like them—a something done with—

"You've got a soft spot for 'em, haven't you, eh?" MacFarlane persisted.

"Yes," said Hector.

Old problems were disappearing now in the North-West Territories, new problems cropping up, old crimes and criminals dying away, new crimes and criminals upon the increase. During the two years which had passed since Hector first met Moon, he had been constantly dealing with these matters, old and new, under desperate conditions. Sheer bull-dog grinding in the face of gigantic difficulties; days and weeks of ceaseless exposure to the cruel cold of mid-winter, the fierce heat of midsummer, drenching rain, stabbing blizzard, rivers in flood-time, trails knee-deep in mud; innumerable arrests, when, single-handed he dragged the wanted man, fighting like a mad dog, from under the very wings of death, in the face of regiments of carbines; other arrests, quiet, subtle, efficient; cases which took inexhaustible patience to bring to a conclusion; cases which leaped from nowhere, demanding instant decision and unhesitating action; and all these cases and arrests, trackings, traps and desperate fights requiring at one time or another, the tip-top pitch of courage, zeal, determination and diplomacy—these things had been Hector's life in those stirring years.

The whiskey-smugglers, haling their stuff across the border for the consumption of Indians and whites, still occupied much of his attention. These were old hands, dealing in old crimes. The worst of the new enemies of the law were the cattle-rustlers, who came in with the ranching industry. Some were whites, most were Indians.

Hector had gradually come to the conclusion that—in the Macleod district at least—the whiskey-runners and cattle-rustlers were operating hand in glove from some central headquarters. Some clever criminal, or group thereof, had organized the two activities into one gigantic business. So far he kept these suspicions to himself, because he had not yet enough evidence to lay before the Inspector. In the meantime, he worked away steadily and in the working gained a reputation for physical strength, courage, determination and a high sense of duty among the officers and men, the settlers and the Indians which was worth far more than any King's ransom.

In the autumn following the receipt of Father Duval's letter he was re-transferred to Fort Macleod. There occurred an incident which nearly wrecked his reputation for all time.

II

"We've got a shipment here for you, Sergeant Adair," announced Randall, the keeper of the Weatherton Company's store at Fort Macleod. Hector walked over to the counter through the crowd of Indians, settlers and policemen.

The trader, when he reached him, was busy with a customer and Hector had to wait. He passed the time in talking to Welland, who was lounging at his elbow—Mr. Joseph Welland now, keener, sprucer, more cordial and certainly more prosperous than ever.

"Well, Hec'—how's the whiskey-running? Putting it down any?" Welland began, while he carelessly picked his teeth with a bit of match.

The question was delivered in a low tone, implying caution.

"So-so," Hector replied vaguely.

Experience had taught him to trust nobody.

"But they're a cunning crowd behind it," he added.

"So they are," Welland agreed emphatically. "Not a doubt of it. That bunch in the Calgary country, now—"

"Is there a bunch working in the Calgary country?" asked Hector innocently.

"You know there is." Welland twinkled. "Guileless angel, ain't you? But, talking of whiskey—"

"Talkin' o' whiskey, are yah?" The trader's oily voice cut in suddenly. "You'll be able to talk o' whiskey for a long time, Sergeant, when you've signed this invoice!"

He winked meaningly at Welland, whose face for one moment betrayed surprise, then became intensely vigilant.

"What's this? What's this?" he exclaimed, half in jest, half in earnest, while his eyes flashed swiftly to the invoice.

Hector read and signed the piece of paper, which told him that Mr. John Adair, of Blenheim County, Ont., had recently shipped to him through Weatherton's chain of stores, evidently as a Christmas gift, one case of Scotch whiskey.

"Well, I'm shot!" Welland remarked. "I'll come an' see you when you've opened it, Hec'. How'll you get it into barracks?"

The last demand, with its veiled insinuation, irritated Hector. But he snubbed Welland by showing no concern.

"Bring it to my quarters next time you're over that way, Randall," he told the store-keeper.

"You're on, Sergeant," Randall leered, rolling his bleary eyes. "An' I hope to drink your health."

"You'll do it in water, then," Hector said quietly. "This whiskey goes to Mother Earth and no-one else."

"Wha-a-t?" Welland cried, amazed. "You're not—?"

"Yes, I am." Hector gathered up his whip and gloves. "I'm going to spill the lot of it, in Randall's presence, too. Nobody's going to say I'm a wholesale drinker myself and down on everyone else drinking."

"But Hec'! It came in a perfectly honest, legal way—"

"Can't help that. Shouldn't have come at all. I can take a drink with others, on the square or in the mess. But I'm not going to stock it myself. I've got too many people ready to take a crack at me and I won't run any chances."

"But Hec', it's a crime to waste—"

"No!" said Hector, real determination in the negative.

Welland drew back, defeated, shrugged his shoulders, and looked at the trader with a sneer.

"Hell!" he exclaimed audibly. "'Course he wants it for himself. That goody-goody stuff is bluff. That's the way with these zealots—no liquor, no! But that just applies to you—not me!"

The tone surprised Hector. He had not expected this thrust from Welland.

"Will you come over and see me get rid of that whiskey?" he flashed.

But Welland only laughed derisively.

"Well, Randall will be witness enough," Hector declared. "Think what you please, and be damned!"

With that, he clanked fiercely out of the store.

The trader exchanged glances with Welland, his florid face growing redder with suppressed delight.

III

Though John had sent the whiskey in a perfectly legitimate way, Hector could not use it, for the reason that, to do his work properly, he must keep up his reputation as an incorruptible enemy of liquor. If he gave way, his enemies would certainly adopt the cynical attitude that Hector, being able to get whiskey for himself whenever he pleased, had nothing to gain by winking at the operations of those less fortunate and so was zealous where he would otherwise have been slack. A better course than destroying the whiskey would have been to ship it straight back to John in Welland's presence; but Hector failed to think of this at the time.

In the late afternoon, Randall drove his sleigh into barracks.

"I got the case outside, Sergeant," he said. "Will I bring it in?"

"No," said Hector. "Dump it on the parade-ground."

Hector took an axe. They went out together.

"Why, Sergeant!" exclaimed Randall, in great alarm. "Yah ain't really goin'—? Ah, say, don't, Sergeant, don't! It's a sinful waste o' the gifts o' Providence, Sergeant—Ah!"

His voice rose to a shriek as Hector reduced the case to a pulp of splintered wood and broken glass.

"Now you tell anyone who ever mentions it what I do to private stock, Randall," said Hector, as he pitched the wreckage into the sleigh. "You understand. You've got to tell the truth. Savvy?"

"A'right, Sergeant, a'right!" Randall shrank back in alarm. "But it's an awful waste o' good Scotch!"

He drove off lamenting.

Hector's mistake had been in securing only one witness to the destruction of the whiskey. He was to pay for it later.

IV

Soon after this, Hector noticed a distinct falling off of the respectful regard held for him by the officers, the men, the civilians. They did not force the change upon him but they hinted at it in a thousand ways.

At a loss for an explanation, he did the wisest thing possible—ignored the change and went on his way in silence.

One day came light, when Inspector Denton summoned him and revealed the truth in a private interview.

"You sent for me, sir?" said Hector, entering the Inspector's sitting-room and saluting smartly.

Inspector Denton was a big man, much inclined to fatness. He had a ruddy face eloquent of good living, a drooping, luxuriant moustache, and an eye-glass which he hardly ever used. Ignorant recruits, judging by appearances, took him for a brainless martinet. As a matter of fact, the strength of a lion, the heart of a Viking and the endurance of a grizzly were hidden beneath his deceptive exterior and when action demanded those who doubted it were rapidly disillusioned.

The Inspector, as Hector entered, was seated by the stove, his tunic open, his feet in gaudy carpet slippers.

"Ah, Adair!" exclaimed the Inspector. "Er—just close the door, will you?"

Hector obeyed.

"I've been—ah—hearing tales about you, Adair," the Inspector began, composedly. "I don't like 'em. My advice is—er—if they're true—stop! I find it difficult to believe 'em, Adair. So I thought I'd talk it over quietly with you—er—alone."

"Tales about you!" Hector saw in a flash that the causes of the mysterious change were about to be revealed to him.

"Very good, sir," he said; and eagerly waited.

"Are they true?"

"I don't know what they are, sir."

"You don't, eh? Umph!"

The Inspector pondered. Then he looked at Hector again.

"Like me to tell you? Well—er—fact is, Adair, they say you're doing a lot of secret drinking, on cases sent from the East an' so on. Very foolish, Adair, if so. Must drink openly or not at all. Ah—makes your work in suppressing the traffic look so—so hypocritical, y'know—besides bringing the Force into disrepute. It's rather hard to explain what I mean but—er—you understand, eh?"

Hector's face crimsoned with passion.

"It's a lie!" he rapped fiercely. And he told the Inspector everything.

"I see!" said Denton thoughtfully. "I see! Well, we must kill this lie—er—immediately, Adair. It's done you a lot of harm—shaken people's confidence in you—er—considerably, very considerably. Even I was—er—-a bit affected. Now let's see. How can we kill it, eh? How can we kill it?"

"I'll kill it, sir!" said Hector decidedly. "I'll kill it, all right!"

"Right you are, Adair! Good example, eh? Even stricter attention to duty—if that were possible—eh? But no violence. Anyway, that's all about it, s'far as I'm concerned. Damn' glad it wasn't true, Adair. Er—settle it quietly, eh? Damn' glad, Adair. Close the door, er—will you, when you go out?"

So this was the cause of the change in feeling! Obviously, it was the work of Randall or Welland, who must at least have started the rumour, whatever their part in its subsequent growth may have been! The story must be killed, the Inspector had said. Well, he would kill it, there and then!

Conscious of his innocence, Hector, for the first time since joining the Police, lost that crowning attribute, self-control.

On fire to avenge his honour, he left the Inspector's and went rapidly over to Weatherton's.

V

The door of the store was dashed open. Fifty startled men, settlers, constables, Indians and half-breeds, turned together towards it, leaving a lane to the counter.

Sergeant Adair came in. They all knew him—but not this Sergeant Adair. The quiet, friendly yet sternly restrained N.C.O. was gone and in his stead was a passionate giant, fists clenched, eyes like knives, lips set and cheeks aflame.

A hush fell on the crowd. It remained for Joe Welland to break it.

The rancher, in a big buffalo coat, was smoking a cigar at the counter. Turning with the rest, he looked at Hector coolly, though with genuine concern, and his voice cut evenly through the silence:

"What's the matter, Adair?"

Hector gripped himself before replying. He was joyfully conscious of the presence of many of his friends, assembled, as if by preordainment, to witness his vindication. There was MacFarlane, staring open-mouthed; Sergeant-Major Whittaker, by the stove, motionless in the act of pulling on his gloves, alert as a bird; Jim Jackson, master of ceremonies at the first Christmas celebration at the fort years before, pausing as he buttoned his fur coat for the trail; Martin Brent, seated on a sack of flour, pipe in mouth, stoically viewing the proceedings; Cranbrook—Corporal Cranbrook now; and a dozen others. For a moment Hector marshalled his words. Then he stepped swiftly into the centre of the room, the silent crowd shrinking before him.

"This is the matter!" he burst out furiously. "Which of you two started these lies about me—you—or you?"

And he pointed an accusing finger, first at Welland, then at Randall.

Deathly silence came again. Men looked at one another. Welland gaped.

"What d'you mean, Hec'? No-one's——

"Oh, yes, they have! Someone's been spreading tales that I've been getting secret whiskey from the East. Don't deny it! I know positively the story's gone 'round for weeks. Am I right, boys?—am I right?"

He flung the appeal to the crowd. They growled assent.

"That's right—that's true."

"Do you hear them?" Hector cried. "There's proof, isn't it? Now, which of you two began it? You know, Welland, that I had a case sent unexpectedly from the East. Randall knows it. You know I said I was going to destroy it. Randall saw me smash it with an axe that same afternoon. Now, no one else in the world knew that whiskey had come to me! Then, which of you spread the story? That's what I want to know."

The crowd waited breathlessly.

Welland calmly flicked the ash from his cigar and smiled.

"Say, you can take this as straight," he asserted. "I've said nothing. If anyone's told any yarns, it's Randall there, not me."

And he glanced with stern contempt at the store-keeper.

Randall started, staring with alarm and consternation.

"Well, say!" he shrilled. "For God's sake, Welland——"

"You shut up!" flashed Welland. Then, quietly, to Hector: "That's your man, Adair."

Hector turned quickly to the crowd.

"Did this man start the rumour?" he demanded, pointing at Randall.

For a moment no-one answered. Fear of a tempest held them silent.

"Did he?"

"I heard it first from him, Sergeant."

The voice, pleasant, careless but assured, was Cranbrook's.

That broke the spell. A chorus of "So did I," "I did, too," rolled solemnly through the crowd.

Hector's fury broke.

MacFarlane raised a husky shout as a dozen bystanders threw themselves on Hector:

"What'you going to do? What'you going to do?"

Jim Jackson rushed into action, shouting, "No, Adair—no!"

Then came a babble:

"Hold him! Hold him!" and a storm of curses——

At the stove Whittaker still stood motionless but smiling quietly——

And Hector burst out of the crowd like a lion from a thicket of spears, grim, silent, deadly. He tossed Jackson and MacFarlane aside with a great sweep of his arm—the powers of twenty men added to his own giant strength in that moment. The trader's frenzied shriek, "Sergeant—for the love of Christ!" he did not heed at all. Seizing Randall in a grip that brought a scream to his lips, he dragged him swiftly across the counter. The scattered crowd closed in. Seeing them, he swung the trader like a flail through the air, dashing them off their feet. In the cleared space, he shook his victim as if he were a sawdust dummy.

"You dog! You dog!" they heard him crying.

Once more the crowd rushed, to save Hector from murder.

"Get back, damn you! He's mine!" Hector roared, pinning the maddened Randall against the counter and staving them off.

"Say you're a liar, you cur! You swine!" he gasped, "Say it or I'll kill you—I'll kill you——"

"I am! I am!" sobbed Randall. "Sergeant—Sergeant——"

"Let him go, Hec'! Let him go!"

MacFarlane's voice gave Hector back his sanity. But, shifting his grip, he tossed the trader, screaming, above his head and held him there, his eyes roving furiously 'round the room.

Then, taking ten great strides, he hurled him crashing but unhurt into a pile of hardware.

"I could kill you!" was in his mind. But instead he said, "Lie there, you dog; lie there!"

Ignoring the crowd utterly—it parted in his path with awed silence—he went to the door, flung it wide open.

The crash of the heavy portal slamming to aroused the crowd to tumult.

VI

Within twenty-four hours the whiskey rumour was as dead as a last year's calendar and Hector was back upon his pedestal.

Mention of his name thenceforward produced this invariable comment:

"Play straight with Adair. He's an easy-goin' bird, but a ring-tailed devil when he's roused!"

Some weeks after the clash with Randall, the Chester affair occurred.

Hector was in charge of the Police herd-camp a few miles from the fort. One morning the detachment shifted to a new site. Chester was a shy, retiring sort of youngster, newly joined. During the move Hector placed him in charge of the tools. As a result, the only axe was left behind. At dusk the loss was discovered and Hector sent the boy off to get it, promising to follow him and aid the search himself.

Darkness fell while he was still some distance from his objective. He caught himself wondering why he did not meet Chester. Reassuring himself with the thought that the boy had perhaps encountered some unforeseen difficulty, he pushed on. But no sign of Chester greeted him. All about the old camp was lifeless and silent.

Returning to camp as rapidly as possible, he hoped to find the missing man there before him. The cook's anxious enquiry disillusioned him:

"Is that you, Chester? And have you got the axe?"

"Turn out, the lot of you," said Hector. "Chester's lost."

Lanterns were lighted and the whole party made an extended search on foot. The results were disappointing. The discovery of the axe added to their alarm.

Hector reported the affair to Inspector Denton, at the fort, who promised to send out a large search party at dawn. To continue the hunt at night would have been futile.

Next morning, in a little hollow as yet untouched by the wind, they found the first clue—a sprinkle of blood, among jumbled hoof-prints—and a wide cast revealed Chester's hat in a clump of bushes. They searched the woods. More evidence of a foreboding character was then quickly gathered and the reason why Chester's horse had not returned was made clear.

Hector himself found the horse. It had been led into the woods, tied to a tree and shot.

And then they found Chester himself. The body was lying in the bottom of a deep ravine, where it had been thrown. The foulest of foul work had been done, for he had been shot in the back at short range.

In the days and weeks that followed, they exhausted every resource, but the murder remained an unsolved mystery.

II

"Beg pardon, sir," said MacFarlane, waylaying Inspector Denton as he passed the guard-room. "The In'juns say they'll talk now. And they want you, with the interpreter, sir, and Sergeant Adair."

The Inspector wheeled quickly.

"Good! Splendid!" he exclaimed. "Is Brent back? Then send a man for 'em right away."

Twenty-four hours previously, Hector had carried out the arrest of a gang of Indian horse-thieves, accused of stealing stock from the 'Lazy G,' an 'outfit' in Montana. They had refused to talk, however, having apparently decided to say nothing whatever until the day of trial. Martin was away and the best linguists in the division had been able to produce no effect. MacFarlane's announcement relieved the Inspector's mind considerably.

When all four—the Inspector, Hector, Martin and MacFarlane—were assembled, they held a consultation outside the guard-room.

"Why in—ah—heavens," said the Inspector, "wouldn't they talk before?"

"Yes—what was the idea?" Hector agreed. "I made everything clear to them. But they wouldn't speak a word."

Martin laughed. He knew the Indian mind better than any of them.

"They got what chaplain call 'guilty conscience,'" he declared. "One thing—they either 'fraid say a word, fear give themselves away, or other thing—they think you have um for bigger job than horse-steal but you won't let on. You bet your boots, that it! They either make confession or give some other feller away. That why they want me an' Inspector. You see—damn quick."

To a number of a dozen, villainous-looking warriors every one of them, the Indians rose to their feet as the Inspector came in. A good deal of parleying then resulted in Bear Sitting Down, who was their leader, being elected to speak for them all. And Martin began.

"Why did you not say what you have to say to Sergeant Adair?"

The Indian looked uncomfortable.

"We would rather talk to you," he said.

"Well, what have you to say?"

Bear Sitting Down glanced nervously 'round the room. The other Indians watched him intently.

"Come," Martin said in his most commanding voice. "Answer quickly. What have you to say?"

Bear Sitting Down shuffled his feet, cleared his throat and at last exclaimed desperately, with the air of a man goaded to action:

"We did not do it. We know we have been arrested on that account. But we had no hand in it."

"No hand in it?"

"No hand in it—none!"

The spokesman's companions seconded him with anxious monosyllables of approval.

Martin's keen eyes flickered.

"Why didn't you tell the Sergeant so when he arrested you?" he asked.

"He told us he was arresting us for horse-stealing. But we know better. We have stolen horses, yes. But we had no hand in the killing of the pony-soldier."

Martin quivered like a dog on an unexpected scent. Otherwise, he betrayed no emotion.

"You are known to have killed him," he said calmly, "and you will all be hanged."

The shot in the dark flashed home.

"No—no—no!" exclaimed Bear Sitting Down. The Indian fear of the rope was evident in his face and he trembled in every limb. "You will not hang us if we tell you who killed him?"

"Not if you speak truth."

Inwardly, Martin was still completely puzzled, but he went on bluffing cleverly.

"I will tell all," said Bear Sitting Down. "The man who did it was Wild Horse. He came to us that night and he said, 'I have killed one of the Shagalasha. I killed his horse also and I threw the body into the ravine.' If you arrest Wild Horse, you will find that this is so."

The mystery solved—at last!

Martin turned swiftly to the other Indians.

"Is this true?" he asked.

"Yes, yes!" they answered eagerly. "It is true—true!"

"Come 'long outside," said Martin to the Inspector, with as much excitement as it was possible for him to show at any time.

"That feller," Martin declared very impressively, "He think you lie, Sergeant. He think you take him up, not for horse-steal—just bluff, that—though he say it true he steal horses, but for murder Constable Chester last spring. An' he say—all say—did not murder Chester. 'You no hang me if I tell who did it?' he ask. 'No hang you,' I say. 'Then,' he say, 'I tell you. Wild Horse kill him!'"

III

A fortnight elapsed before Hector was able to attempt the arrest of Wild Horse. The Indian had taken alarm with the apprehension of the horse-thieves and had left the reserve. Sooner or later, Hector knew, he would return, thinking the storm blown over. It behooved the Police to be ready to take him when that time came. They placed the reserve under the observation of Liver-eating John, a half-breed scout, whose orders were immediately to report to Hector any news concerning the whereabouts of Wild Horse.

So the fortnight dragged by. Then, in great haste, one afternoon, came Liver-eating John.

"Wild Horse, he sneak in 'bout noon," he told Hector. "Me see um—self. He be there p'raps two days. Hide in brother's lodge. Go, get him, quick!"

Within fifteen minutes, Hector and his men were on the trail.

Among those who had recently committed themselves to the baby business of ranching in Western Canada was

Colonel Stern, a veteran of the Indian Mutiny and several other wars. Failing fortunes had driven him from the Army to seek a livelihood south of Fort Macleod. But, though his military service had ceased, his interest in all wearers of the Queen's uniform was as bright as ever. He kept open house for all ranks of the Police and it was an understood thing that any redcoat passing that way, on duty or otherwise, was to stop off at Colonel Stern's ranch. As the place stood on the edge of the reserve wherein Wild Horse was lurking, Hector headed for Colonel Stern's as a matter of course.

The Colonel—tall, gray-headed, hook-nosed, weather-beaten, with bushy brows, a heavy military moustache and eyes like rapiers—met them at the door as they loped into the yard at dusk, smiling a welcome and holding out his hand.

"And how are you, Sergeant?" he asked. "Looking like a young stallion, as usual. I'm not going to ask what brings you here, because that's none of my business."

Hector took him aside, nevertheless, and explained.

"I see," the Colonel commented. "Well, it's too late to catch him tonight, Adair. He'd surely get away in the dark. Besides, there's a storm coming up. It will be a wet night—no night for lying in the open. Catch 'em at dawn—that's sound tactics. They won't be stirring then, especially with the rain coming down, and you can take the whole camp by surprise. Come along—supper now, stay here tonight and you'll be fit for anything in the morning."

It was raining, as the Colonel had prophesied, when they turned out, a thin, penetrating, all-day drizzle, and the sky, just lightening, was heavy with an unbroken pall of dense grey cloud. Such weather, all in all, was admirable for their purpose. Half an hour's careful scouting brought them within sight of the teepees they sought—a ghostly group in the wet desolation. The question was—in which lodge was Wild Horse?

At this moment, they found an Indian boy, who willingly pointed out the teepee occupied by The Gopher, headman of the band. In order to comply with the custom of the Police it was necessary that Hector should inform The Gopher of his intentions.

The Gopher was instantly at the door when Hector sent the small boy into the teepee to awaken him. Speaking the Indian's own tongue, Hector rapidly explained his mission and was relieved to find that the Gopher, far from offering any objection, took the matter philosophically and himself pointed out the lodge in which Wild Horse was hiding.

"Keep everyone in their teepees," Hector went on, "until we go. Then there will be small likelihood of trouble."

The Gopher agreed. Hector ordered the constable with the horses up to a position close to Wild Horse's lodge. The others he placed one on each side, ready to seize the murderer should he attempt escape by crawling under the flap. For the last time, obedient to one of the greatest principles of the Mounted Police, he cautioned the men on no account to draw their revolvers. Then, removing his great-coat, he boldly entered the teepee alone.

For a moment unable to see anything, he shortly became aware of the presence of at least a dozen Indians, who sat up in their blankets and stared at him anxiously.

"What do you want?" one of them asked, bristling defiance.

Hector pushed back the door of the lodge still further. The cold light, streaming in, clearly revealed his uniform.

"I have come for Wild Horse," he answered.

The wanted Indian glared shiftily at the speaker over the edge of his blanket.

"You hear me, Wild Horse?" Hector queried. "I say I have come for you. You know what that means. I am waiting."

"I will not come," answered Wild Horse.

"What do you mean?" said Hector sternly.

The Indians had learned to dread that tone. They stirred uneasily.

"I will not come!" repeated Wild Horse.

The others broke into a loud murmur of applause. Some of the bolder threw off their blankets and reached for their rifles. Hector caught the sound of angry voices at his back. A hostile crowd was gathering outside. The Gopher had failed, either through weakness or treachery, to maintain control. Hector remembered that they were only four white men among at least a hundred Indians. The least misstep, lack of tact or wavering in courage, might have fatal consequences.

He fixed the murderer with penetrating eyes.

"I say that you are to come," he said. "Do not look so at me—I will not have it. And do not attempt to resist or it will be the worse for you."

In reply, Wild Horse bounded suddenly to his feet, a knife in his hand. The other Indians, muttering fierce threats, stood up behind him. A row of levelled rifles confronted Hector.

"Get out of this lodge!" said Wild Horse.

Instantly Hector closed. A wrench twisted the knife from the Indian's hand. Seizing him, he exerted a supreme effort of his great strength, whirled him off his feet and threw him bodily out of the lodge. Before the murderer's friends could pull a trigger, Hector was also outside.

But it was 'out of the frying-pan into the fire.'

A crowd apparently representing every grown man in camp, to say nothing of women and boys, was thickly clustered round the teepee. The men were all armed and many of them were actually covering the two constables.

One glance revealed all this to Hector; another, that Wild Horse had been promptly and efficiently handcuffed by his men, who held the murderer between them.

What now?

"Take him out of this," Hector ordered coolly. To the crowding Indians, he gave the stern command, "Stand back!"

They answered with a wild yell and one overwhelming rush.

In the furious struggle that resulted, only the intervening bodies of the nearest Indians prevented the policemen from being shot. To hang on to Wild Horse and to beat their assailants off without drawing a weapon—these two thoughts occupied Hector's mind exclusively. He could trust his men—through it all, they clung to Wild Horse like grim death. Meanwhile, all three were knocked down a dozen times, trampled on, beaten with rifles, bitten, throttled, kicked. When opportunity offered, Hector gathered his failing breath and bellowed for The Gopher.

"Give us Wild Horse!" yelled the Indians, pulling and dragging at the policemen. "Let him go!"

"He is our prisoner," answered Hector. "Where is The Gopher?"

So, like a football scrum, the three undaunted redcoats carried the crowd with them to the horses. The mob raved on. The crash of their carbines pierced the uproar.

"Put up your gun, will you!" Hector bawled, as the constable in charge of the horses, a young fellow and inexperienced, drew his revolver.

Then suddenly, at this crisis, came comparative quiet and The Gopher pushed his way forward.

"Where have you been?" Hector demanded. "What do you mean by allowing this to go on?"

The Gopher pretended not to hear. Instead, he bent his energies towards quelling the riot. Presently Hector found himself beside his horses, the prisoner and escort with him, the crowd, visibly subdued, falling back with lowered rifles and the shamefaced Gopher at his side.

"They know they've done a serious thing," Hector thought.

His troubles were obviously over. What plain men call sheer 'guts' had carried the day, as they so often do—as, with savages, they always do.

Hector struck while the iron was hot.

"Now that you have recovered your senses," he said to the hangdog assembly, "I have a word to say to you. You have committed a grave crime. You have tried to stop the arrest of one of your number by a Mounted Policeman. That is wrong, as you know. And it is also quite useless. You see that we are not afraid of you. When the Mounted Police come for any man, white or red, he has got to come, and we will see that he does come, let a thousand rifles come between. Wild Horse will get a fair trial, you know that. As for you," here he turned to The Gopher, who hung his head, "you have disgraced yourself. Instead of helping us with your authority, you stood aside. The Mounted Police have always treated you well—and this is how you repay us! You are unworthy of your trust. Is it not so?"

"It is so," The Gopher muttered sullenly.

"If you have any explanation to make, you must come to Fort Macleod. And let us have no more of this because, I tell you again, when the Mounted Police come for any man, he has got to come and it is no use resisting."

A moment later, with Wild Horse between them, Hector and his little party rode slowly out of the camp. In recognition of their superior authority, courage and determination, the Indians fell back before them as they passed, lowering their rifles with a gesture that was a salute.

IV

On the night following the lodgment of Wild Horse in the cells at Fort Macleod, Hector was called hurriedly to Inspector Denton's quarters.

Three men occupied the Inspector's parlour when Hector got there—Wild Horse, Martin and Denton himself. The air was tense with drama and breathed secrecy. The windows had been carefully screened and the key-hole blocked with paper, measures insisted on by Wild Horse, who was in deadly fear of spies or eavesdroppers. The lamp had also been turned down and placed out of the direct line of the windows. The dim light remaining fell on the faces of the men around the table with an unearthly glow. All in all, the place might well have been a noisome den devoted to the most fearful crimes and its occupants conspirators of the deepest dye.

"That you, Adair?" The reassuring voice of the Inspector greeted Hector. "Right. This may be a—er—long business, so you'd better sit down. Now, Martin, tell him to go ahead—slowly. I can understand him myself then."

"What have you to say?" demanded Martin, using the Indian's own language and speaking with the severity he always adopted toward redskin criminals.

Wild Horse glanced fearfully round the room and finally broke silence in a voice little louder than a whisper. He spoke very rapidly. The Inspector attempted to stem the tide with an indignant "Go slow! Dash it, go slow!" but the Indian paid no heed and even Martin raised a hand to silence his superior. Wild Horse ceased at last.

"Well, what's he say?" the Inspector enquired.

"He want to know," Martin replied, "if he tell all trut', we no' string him up. He want to know, if he give way man who got him shoot Chester, we save him from that man. We promise and he say he talk. We no promise, then he no talk."

The Inspector entered into a long explanation of the laws governing evidence and trial, admonishing Wild Horse, for his own good, to talk.

Followed a vehement discussion between Martin and the murderer, which Martin finally boiled down to one brief statement:

"He no' like talk. He ver' much afraid white man."

"Tell him the whole Force will protect him if necessary."

More vehement discussion; then Martin said:

"Good! He talk."

Bit by bit, with many frightened starts and pauses, Wild Horse unfolded the truth. Thanks to the hesitating manner of the telling, Hector followed it with comparative ease, first with interest, then with incredulity, rising step by step to understanding, conviction and certainty. Here was new light on dark places, here, in a few moments, the perplexities of years were made plain.

Said Wild Horse:

"I did kill the pony-soldier found dead in the ravine last spring. But I was bribed to do it by a white man; and I was mad with fire-water. This white man, he used often to give me that poison. He knew I had broken the law several times and would never dare to betray him, so he gave it me without fear, not only for myself but for others. I would carry it into camp in all sorts of ways—many gallons of it. We would pay him for it with buffalo-robes and other pelts, even with stolen horses and cattle. He never gave the whiskey to anyone but me, as far as I know. He made sure that he would not be betrayed in that manner. He is cunning as a wolf. And I have made him rich.

"Well, one day he sent for me and gave me a lot of fire-water and he told me he would give me lots more if I would do something for him. And he added, if I would not it would be the worse for me. So I said I would obey him, because I was afraid. Then he told me I must kill this man, the Sergeant here."

And Wild Horse pointed straight at Hector.

"I knew the Sergeant—have often seen him. I was afraid, so I said I would do it. I went to the herd-camp and hid all day under a tarpaulin. Just before the Police moved on to a new place, I heard the Sergeant tell one of the men he would go with them and come back later alone. So, when the Police were not looking, I crept out and hid in a good place near the trail. I waited till nearly dark. Then I saw a man coming along. I thought it was the Sergeant. Had he not said he was coming back alone? Besides, I could not see his face at that hour. I shot him dead. When I looked at him, I saw my mistake. But I put him on his horse and led him away; and the rest you know. Then I returned to my lodge. I wanted to hide in some other part of the country but I knew that if you found me absent you would suspect me. So I stayed there. The chinook wiped out all traces, so I had nothing to fear from that. And you did not suspect me.

"I thought it was all forgotten. Then you came and arrested Bear Sitting Down and the rest. That made me afraid. I had foolishly told Bear Sitting Down what I had done, while still drunk, and I thought you had arrested him because of that and I feared he would betray me. So I ran away. When I thought it was safe I came back. And then the Sergeant came himself and took me. That is all. I would not have killed the young man if I had not been drunk and mad for more fire-water and in the power of that bad white man. I swear that is true. Now go you and arrest him. He——"

"Yes?" said Martin, encouragingly. "Who is he?"

Wild Horse described his master.

"It's Welland!" Hector exclaimed, "Joe Welland!"

V

There was no question of it. The man who had bribed Wild Horse to attempt Hector's murder was Welland.

"Why, it's impossible!" Inspector Denton declared, when Hector explained. "Welland? He's one of the—ah—wealthiest, most influential, most respected men in the country. He would have no object——"

Hector shook his head. The time had come for him to unmask the man he had long suspected but against whom he had hitherto been unable to amass enough evidence. Wild Horse had pieced the puzzle together for him.

"I'll tell you what I think of Joe Welland, sir!" he said tersely. "He's the biggest horse-thief, cattle-rustler and whiskey-smuggler this side the boundary. Yes, sir," as the Inspector voiced a mild protest, "that's so. Oh, I've suspected him for a long, long time. We've tried to clear the district of those crimes, sir, and made some progress, too; and yet can't completely stop it. Well, sir, some time ago it struck me that the reason why we weren't able to stamp out the business was that it was being run from a central headquarters. This headquarters kept itself well informed of our movements, so that it could direct operations with the best chances of success. It kept itself well informed, with the result that, capture as many of its tools as we please, we could never nab the men on top. This pointed to careful organization, employing men over whom it had a definite hold only and letting those men into no matter that did not directly concern them. The small men had no idea of the scope of the gang employing them, nor, in fact, any knowledge of the chief men, to say nothing of their own comrades. Each was just a cog in the machine, doing the little job assigned them. When arrested, they gave no evidence of value because they hadn't any. So we just jailed them as men convicted of a small share in the big game and went on working in the dark as before."

"That sounds plausible," the Inspector asserted, a little doubtfully. "But—er—what about Welland?"

"Why, sir,"—Hector was aflame now with the conviction that they were on the verge of a big thing—"we know how easily Welland became wealthy, apparently without effort. All sorts of evidence, too small to arrest him on but still damning, gradually brought me to suspect him. His herds of horses—new buildings—lands—where did they come from? The horses and cattle were stolen by gangs of Indians and whites, who did not know they were working under that man but simply delivered them to men who in turn handed them over to him—men in his power. Selling these herds, he made money. But the greater amount by far was made from the sale of robes, horses and cattle received in exchange for whiskey run into the country by his organization. That's how he got wealthy, I'm certain of it now. I could tell you a thousand little things that show why I suspect him, sir, but it would take a long time. Meanwhile——"

"Well, meanwhile—what?"

"We have evidence enough from this Indian, sir. Welland bribed him to shoot me. Why? Because I've been too hot on the trail of his whiskey-runners for the past few years! He was afraid I might get too near soon, so he thought he'd better put me out of the way first. What more easy than to have this done by an Indian in his power—an Indian who wouldn't dare to give him away if caught? That's why he picked Wild Horse. If Wild Horse hadn't made a mistake, I'd be dead now—and my suspicions with me! Look at the evidence we've against him, from Wild Horse alone, sir!"

The Inspector pondered.

"Er—about this idea that he was out to finish you, Adair. And—ah—about this organization of which he's the—ah—chief. Can you give me an example of the sort of thing that made you suspicious?"

Hector was ready for this.

"Yes, I can, sir. You remember when I settled that whiskey story and—well, dealt with Randall, the man who started it?"

A flicker of a smile played over the Inspector's face.

"Yes, I do," he replied.

"Well, it comes to me now that that was started to discredit me—perhaps to make you think I wasn't to be trusted, sir, and get you to take me off the whiskey-runners altogether. If Welland is what I think he is, that's just what he'd do. Now, Welland was the only man except Randall who knew that whiskey had been shipped to me. If he had power over Randall, he could make him circulate those yarns and take the blame later. Finding that the scheme wouldn't work, he next thinks of putting me out for good by getting Wild Horse to shoot me. I'm certain if we get Randall here now, sir, and tell him we know part of the truth and want the rest, he'll give it to us. Being in Welland's power, as I believe, he'll welcome a chance to knife him. Besides, he's a coward, and will think more of saving his own skin than of anything else."

The Inspector was slowly but surely marshalling the facts and was almost finally convinced.

"That's an idea, too," he declared. "But Welland's always been a good friend of ours, Adair. He's—ah—respected everywhere and——"

"He's made a fortune out of that sham respectability, sir," Hector said. "His friendship was carefully planned from the time we first came in—I'm sure of that now. He was probably whiskey-trading as a side-line when we arrived and, instead of really welcoming us, he hated to see us come. After that he could only carry on with safety by doing it secretly, while he played the friendly respectable on the surface. That tune went down well with the decent people in the country; and how were newcomers like ourselves to know him for what he really was? The only man who could possibly succeed at the head of the organization I've described, sir, was a man we all considered respectable—I saw that when I first became suspicious that such an organization actually existed. Welland is thought to be one of the most respectable in the country, as you've said—and tonight what Wild Horse has said leaves me absolutely convinced."

The Inspector looked Hector in the eyes.

"I believe you're right!" he said. "Send out for Randall."

VI

Hector's estimate of Randall proved absolutely correct. He told them all he knew.

"Ya've caught me with the goods, I guess," he said, nervously twisting his big hands and rolling his bloodshot eyes, "so I may's well 'fess up. But for God's sake, don't give me away to Welland. That feller, he's a hound o' hell, Mr. Denton. He beats that there squaw o' his——"

"Beats his squaw, Randall?" queried the Inspector, astonished.

"Yessir, beats the hide off'n her. There ain't many knows that but I know it—blast him! An' he's——"

"That'll do. Get on with your story," the Inspector said.

"Well, sir, he come to me an' he says, 'You got to start a story against Adair,' he says. 'He's been interferin' a sight too much in my business lately—' Hector flashed a triumphant look to the Inspector, a look that plainly said 'I told you so!'—'an' I want him broke. I want him ruined!' he says. 'That case o' whiskey,' he says, 'that gives us what we want.' Then he tells me I gotta tell everyone Sergeant Adair was as bad a whiskey-runner as any in the North-West, that he was gettin' whiskey up reg'lar from th' East—you know all about it, Sergeant! I wouldn't 'a' done it, I wouldn't, Sergeant, that's straight—but that human devil, he made me."

"He's got you, too, eh?" the Inspector interjected. "What had you done, Randall—theft or murder?"

"Eh? Eh?" Randall jerked, jaw dropping.

The shaft had struck him fair and square.

"It wasn't anythin' like that, Mr. Denton, I swear. That's—"

"Look here," the Inspector rapped. "You're lying! You'll deny you've traded whiskey for him next!"

"Whiskey?" Randall's face was ghastly. "Mr. Denton, for God's sake——"

"I knew it!" the Inspector exclaimed remorselessly. "Hand in glove with that Indian there, too, I'll bet!"

Wild Horse jumped uneasily. Randall cast a frightened glance in that direction.

"Ah, Inspector," he cried, desperately. "No—I never seen that feller before. That's Gospel true! I'll admit I smuggled whiskey, but——"

Hector cut him short.

"You see, sir," he said to Denton, "he's one of the minor cogs in the machine. Wild Horse is another. Both work under Welland—neither knows the other from Adam!"

The Inspector nodded.

"Tell us what happened after your scandal-mongering failed," he ordered.

Randall hesitated—then made the plunge.

"Well, sir, 't was like this. Welland come to me one Sunday, 'bout three weeks after Sergeant Adair treated me so rough. He reckoned the game had failed. Sergeant Adair was still workin' on the whiskey business and was more of a hero than ever. Welland was rip-snortin' mad—said he'd like to have Adair shot. 'Adair ain't done nothin' to shoot him for,' I says. 'Oh, hasn't he?' says Welland, 'He's done more'n you think. Always pokin' his nose into other people's affairs.' That's all he said an' he never mentioned Adair ag'in. He never said nothin' to me 'bout usin' Wild Horse to shoot the Sergeant. I never knowd nothin' 'bout that."

"All right, Randall. We'll believe you," said the Inspector. "At any rate, Adair, he confirms Wild Horse's statement to this extent—that Welland actually threatened to settle you. After the whiskey fiasco, he thought—ah—murder a better scheme than any. Taking all the evidence, Adair, we've got about enough to give him—ah—at least ten years. Frankly, I—ah—think you've landed the biggest fish and—er—uncovered the biggest thing you've come across since the Force started. This will cause a sensation! And—er—if you bring him in and he's found guilty, I—ah—shouldn't be at all surprised if it meant—ah—promotion. In the meantime, we must collar him as quickly as possible. Think you'd better try the arrest? It might be—ah—rather risky, for you!"

"That's just why I want to do it, sir!" Hector declared, with all the emphasis possible. "This is a personal fight between Welland and myself. He's made it so; and I must see it through. Besides, he's my meat, anyway. I trailed him. I showed him up. I must see it through. And I'd rather do it single-handed, sir, if you don't mind."

The Inspector leisurely filled his pipe.

"I—er—appreciate your viewpoint, Sergeant," he said at last. "By George, if any one should arrest him, it's you! Where is he?"

"At home," Randall interrupted. "I know, 'cos he went back there yesterday."

"Right. Handle it your own way, Adair. You'd better start at once, though there's no particular hurry. You're sure to catch him by surprise. But do as you please. It's your hand."

"I won't leave anything to chance, sir," replied Hector. "I'll start wow."

"Right." The Inspector lighted his pipe at the lamp. "I'll expect him within twenty-four hours. And, oh—as you pass the guard-room, tell 'em to send over an escort for two prisoners. What's that, Randall? Why, of course you're going behind the bars, too, my good man. You surely don't imagine—Good luck—ah—to you, Adair."

"Thank you, sir."

Hector saluted and was gone.

The Inspector had said there was 'no particular hurry.' Hector himself believed that there was 'no particular hurry.' Both were lamentably wrong.

One of Welland's spies had overheard every syllable of the discussion in the Inspector's parlour and, before Hector had saddled up, had left Fort Macleod two good miles behind and was galloping hot-foot for Welland's to warn him of his danger.

VII

On clearing the barracks and turning his horse into the trail to Welland's ranch, sixty miles distant, Hector saw that the moon was rising among the scattered clouds above the distant foothills, and he studied his watch by its radiance: eight o'clock exactly. He planned to reach Welland's before dawn. Setting a brisk pace, if all went well, he should have his enemy under arrest within six or seven hours. The trail was so clearly revealed that he could safely proceed at almost any speed. He settled down for the long ride.

As he went, he found himself unable to put out of his mind the night's startling revelations. Having long suspected Welland of whiskey-smuggling, horse-stealing and cattle-rustling, confirmation of these suspicions caused him no surprise. But that Welland had plotted his disgrace and afterwards his death came home with unexpected force. He saw now that, from the time when they first met, until that moment, Welland's feelings towards him were nothing but sham, maintained for purposes of his own. Welland had recognized him long ago as a man who would probably become dangerous and had gone out of his way from the first to hoodwink him—to produce in Hector's mind an impression strongly favourable to himself. As with Hector, so with the Force generally, to a lesser degree, and so also with the civilians of the district. To discover that Welland's friendship had always been false, that, while apparently well disposed toward him, the rancher had long been plotting against him and had actually attempted to murder him—this was a very bitter pill.

Running over various incidents, Hector, now that his had been opened, could see traces of Welland's deceit everywhere. The warmth with which he had condemned all evil-doers and especially all whiskey-traders when he first came to Fort Macleod had been nothing but hypocrisy, to blind them to his own misdoings. The energy with which he had worked to make their first Christmas a success had been born, not of generous good feeling, but a selfish desire to increase his own popularity with the Force and thus lend further concealment to his real character. He had pushed Hector into prominence on that occasion simply to strengthen the latter's good opinion. The interest he had always shown in Hector's work—as when he enquired so tenderly after the progress he was making with the whiskey-runners when they met in Weatherton's store—that, too, was a sham, an attempt to win useful information. One by one, Hector took these things from their dusty pigeon-holes, examined them in this new light and added them to the damning evidence he had collected against Welland.

So much for that friendship!

Other matters came back to him, bits of evidence of which he had just hinted to Inspector Denton. There was, for instance, the fright displayed by Welland when the party of Police arrived unexpectedly at his house on the way to 'Red-hot' Dan's and asked for shelter. The rancher had been so startled that one might have almost fancied him anticipating arrest. And later, when he endeavored to scare them with wonderful stories of the desperate character of the wanted man—what was this but a sign that he was in league with the trader and desired to gain time to warn him and secure his escape into U.S. territory, while the Police returned to Fort Macleod for reinforcements? They had found 'Red-hot' Dan ready for them, even as it was, and Hector suspected, now, that Welland had obtained means at least to warn him in time to put up a resistance. Hector remembered the shrieks he had heard on the way to the

Sun Dance and knew that Randall's tale of Welland beating his squaw was true. It was then that Welland had shown him the buffalo skull used by the smugglers—an effort, that, to put him off the scent. The man had been cunning as the devil; but not cunning enough. These things, together, betrayed him at last as a liar, a traitor, a brute, an arch-criminal.

And it was with this man—no petty law-breaker but a foeman worthy of his steel—that Hector had his quarrel. He was almost glad that such a man had chosen him as a special enemy, had in fact forced him to take up as a personal fight what otherwise would have been only a matter of duty. He leaped to meet the challenge. 'This is a personal fight between Welland and myself,' he had told the Inspector. 'He's made it so; and I must see it through. Besides, he's my meat, anyway. I trailed him. I showed him up. I must see it through. And I'd rather do it single-handed....' The words came back to him as he rushed through the night and he looked forward, keen as mustard, to the moment which should bring them face to face, in the struggle which had been approaching year after year and was now at hand....

He was so absorbed in these pleasant anticipations that, in spite of the bright moonlight, he failed to notice a hole in the trail. His horse, half asleep, though cantering, was as blind as himself. Somersaulting heels over head, horse and rider fell. The horse stumbled wildly to its feet. But Hector lay stunned.

And the spy ahead went galloping on.

VIII

At three o'clock in the morning Joe Welland woke from a sweet dream to find his squaw beside him. On the arrest of Wild Horse, he had sent Lizzie to Fort Macleod to watch and report developments. Her return was now sufficient evidence to tell him that something momentous had happened.

A horrible fear swept over him and, sitting up in bed, he frantically ordered her to speak.

In her halting English, Lizzie obeyed. Long a familiar and pathetic figure in barracks, no-one had suspected her and she had been able to maintain a close watch on Wild Horse's prison. When she saw him brought to Inspector Denton's quarters, she guessed that vital developments would follow. Going round to the Inspector's kitchen, she begged for food. Mrs. Denton knew her quite well and thought her harmless. She gave her a seat in the kitchen and a bite of supper. Lizzie, when left for a moment alone, slipped into a hiding-place under the stairs, whence she overheard everything going on in the parlour. As soon as she learned that Sergeant Adair was to start for Welland's, she escaped from barracks unobserved, mounted her pony, which was tethered in a gully not far off, and had ridden over the sixty miles at the best speed possible.

Then she gave the rancher full details of the conference.

It was typical of Welland that he had no word of thanks for the woman who had dared and endured so much for his sake. Day in and day out, through the years, he had used her as a slave, working her to exhaustion and often flogging her. Yet, with the dumb devotion characteristic of the Indian woman, she had borne it all, content to suffer his injustice if only she might dedicate her life to him. And now, in his great need, when she might have left him to the fate he well deserved, when circumstances had offered her an opportunity for retribution, she had unhesitatingly done her best to save his wretched hide. Years of selfish brutality had made him incapable of gratitude for the greatest of services, and he would have regarded the sacrifice of her life for him as a matter of course.

It did not take him long to see that flight was his only refuge. His day was done. The Police—represented, in his view, by Hector—had at last unmasked him, had gathered conclusive evidence against him and were at that very moment on their way to take him. When they had him safely in jail, he realized, they would set about gathering more information. With the Chester murder against him, it would be at least a life sentence. To attempt to bluff it out was madness. If the Police laid hands on him, he was doomed. The United States boundary was only a few miles away. Once on American soil, he could quickly hide himself so that not even the Yankees could find him. After that, he could begin life over again somewhere. This life, the life of Mr. Joseph Welland, rancher—had crumbled to pieces round him and only instant action could save him from burial in the ruins.

A man of quick decisions, his mind was at once made up. Jumping out of bed, he began to dress, throwing instructions at Lizzie the while.

"And don't make a noise, or I'll kill you," he adjured.

Fear lent him swiftness and strength. Already, he fancied he heard Hector's voice, summoning him to surrender. Hector! At thought of him, Welland was possessed with fury. To Hector, he knew, he owed his downfall. With infinite patience and cunning, beginning years before Hector's arrival, the rancher had built up a criminal machine of amazing efficiency, a machine which had made him rich. He had hidden his own connection with the machine so cleverly that, as time went on, he began to consider himself absolutely safe. One by one his vassals were jailed but no evil consequences for himself resulted.

He had taken good care, from the first, to see that they were men who knew it best to keep their mouths shut. So, to all the world, he had continued to be Joseph Welland, most respectable of ranchers. The world might have lingered on in this illusion for Heaven knows how long, at least until the day when, made wealthy by the machine, he might have scrapped it and became truly respectable. That day, of late, had seemed near; and he looked forward to it, since, to do him justice, he was not a master-criminal for the love of it nor a secret associate with low-down whites and Indians for any love he bore them. That day had seemed near; and now, thanks to Hector, it was gone forever.

It was no satisfaction to him at this moment to recall that from the first he had recognized the quiet, immensely keen young giant as a dangerous factor. But the knowledge that he had been unable to maintain Hector in ignorance of his real character, that he had failed to realize until too late that Hector was on his track, and that, when realization came, he had made so poor a job of his attempt to 'settle' him—this knowledge tortured him.

Well, he would see to it that he was not taken by Sergeant Adair or any other Mounted Policeman! If he hurried, he might still get away to such a start that no-one could overtake him. But he must hurry. Hector could not have been far behind Lizzie in leaving Fort Macleod.

The black horse stolen from 'Lazy G' was the best in the stable! He ran out into the moonlight to saddle him.

IX

Hector's struggling return to consciousness ended when he felt something soft and warm against his hand and found his horse anxiously nuzzling him. For a minute or two he was powerless to think or move. The moon and stars went wheeling weirdly round and round, while a sticky stream coursed slowly down his cheek. Feeling horribly sick and weak, he yielded to an intense desire to sleep and closed his eyes again.

Meanwhile, precious time was flying.

From this condition he recovered with a start and a dawning sense that something important was hanging in the balance. His next thought was to get to his feet; but, when he tried to rise, agonizing pains shot through him, dragging a groan from his lips and forcing beads of sweat to his face. He sat up gasping, teeth clenched. The spasm past, he tried again, got to his knees, then, catching at the stirrup, dragged himself slowly up and so at last to a standing position. Had he not had the saddle to cling to, he would certainly have fallen. As it was, he reeled drunkenly and only the dim knowledge that he must pull himself together gave him the power to hold on.

So, as he hung there, everything came back to him. He remembered that he was on the trail to Welland's to arrest the rancher. Then he saw that the saddle was twisted to one side and the oak cantle broken. The horse, too, was cut and grimy about the knees and blood had dried in its nostrils. Next he realized that his tunic had been ripped up the back and was hanging in shreds. His hat was gone, his face covered with dirt, the clammy streams on his cheeks were blood, flowing from wounds in his forehead. Then he recollected the fall. The horse had apparently put its forefoot in a hole and turned a somersault. In the fall, pinned beneath the horse, he had been torn along the ground. Gradually he realized that had he not been exceptionally strong, he would have been killed by the fall, in which he had been dragged twenty feet.

As things were he was in no condition to go on. Even the iron code of the Mounted Police had no quarrel with a man who yielded when in such a state as Hector found himself. But his first thought was for the business in hand. The moon was going down. His watch had stopped at three o'clock. Then probably he had lain there hours afterwards. In desperate haste, he set about making up for lost time.

The whole secret of his reputation was revealed in that crisis.

He was sick and sore and his brain was whirling like a top. Yet somehow he twisted the saddle back into its rightful position, thanking God that his horse had remained faithfully beside him throughout, thus enabling him to complete his journey on horseback instead of on foot. Then he got somehow into the saddle, somehow started the horse and so, the reins twisted round his hands, while his fingers clung to the mane and he held on from hip to heel, urged gradually into a steady gallop.

"Am I in time? Am I in time?"

Drumming in his head with the beat of hoofs, that was the only thought he could retain.

The rest of the ride was sheer torture, without dimensions of time or distance. The road staggered under him, the horse rocked, the moon, now almost out, did idiotic things. Every shooting pain, every bump, went through him with terrible violence, his desire to end this agony and get to grips with Welland became a consuming fire.

"Am I in time? Am I in time?"

More dead than alive, he pounded into Welland's yard at last. Dawn was gilding the mountains. The shack showed only one feeble light. In a daze, biting back the cry of torment beating at his lips, he slid to the ground.

Now!

He opened the door cautiously. From Welland's bedroom, the light burned dimly. Hector entered.

At the entrance to the room, he found confusion everywhere. A dark form crouched, moaning, in a corner. She looked up at him—Lizzie! The sight gave him a nasty shock, for he fancied her at Fort Macleod.

Suddenly possessed of a vague uneasiness, he strode quickly in. Welland, acting on some strange freak, had left a message for him under the lamp on the table. He snatched it up and read:

"You have won this time. But I will win yet. I owe you my ruin and, if it takes me twenty years, I'll get even. Remember, I'll get even, if it takes me twenty years."

The threat was lost on Hector—at any other time he would have laughed at it. But now he turned swiftly to Lizzie.

"Where is Joe?" he demanded.

Surely, surely Welland had not escaped him, after all that had passed?

"Where is Joe?" he repeated fiercely.

Lizzie laughed in mad triumph.

"He gone—hour ago! You no' catch him. He over the medicine-line!"

Hector rapped an inward oath of agony. White man—ghastly in the lamp-light, with pale, bloody face, and tattered scarlet—and Indian, they stared at each other.

8

Old problems were disappearing now in the North-West Territories, new problems cropping up, old crimes and criminals dying away, new crimes and criminals upon the increase. During the two years which had passed since Hector first met Moon, he had been constantly dealing with these matters, old and new, under desperate conditions. Sheer bull-dog grinding in the face of gigantic difficulties; days and weeks of ceaseless exposure to the cruel cold of mid-winter, the fierce heat of midsummer, drenching rain, stabbing blizzard, rivers in flood-time, trails knee-deep in mud; innumerable arrests, when, single-handed he dragged the wanted man, fighting like a mad dog, from under the very wings of death, in the face of regiments of carbines; other arrests, quiet, subtle, efficient; cases which took inexhaustible patience to bring to a conclusion; cases which leaped from nowhere, demanding instant decision and unhesitating action; and all these cases and arrests, trackings, traps and desperate fights requiring at one time or another, the tip-top pitch of courage, zeal, determination and diplomacy—these things had been Hector's life in those stirring years.

The whiskey-smugglers, haling their stuff across the border for the consumption of Indians and whites, still occupied much of his attention. These were old hands, dealing in old crimes. The worst of the new enemies of the law were the cattle-rustlers, who came in with the ranching industry. Some were whites, most were Indians.

Hector had gradually come to the conclusion that—in the Macleod district at least—the whiskey-runners and cattle-rustlers were operating hand in glove from some central headquarters. Some clever criminal, or group thereof, had organized the two activities into one gigantic business. So far he kept these suspicions to himself, because he had not yet enough evidence to lay before the Inspector. In the meantime, he worked away steadily and in the working gained a reputation for physical strength, courage, determination and a high sense of duty among the officers and men, the settlers and the Indians which was worth far more than any King's ransom.

In the autumn following the receipt of Father Duval's letter he was re-transferred to Fort Macleod. There occurred an incident which nearly wrecked his reputation for all time.

II

"We've got a shipment here for you, Sergeant Adair," announced Randall, the keeper of the Weatherton Company's store at Fort Macleod. Hector walked over to the counter through the crowd of Indians, settlers and policemen.

The trader, when he reached him, was busy with a customer and Hector had to wait. He passed the time in talking to Welland, who was lounging at his elbow—Mr. Joseph Welland now, keener, sprucer, more cordial and certainly more prosperous than ever.

"Well, Hec'—how's the whiskey-running? Putting it down any?" Welland began, while he carelessly picked his teeth with a bit of match.

The question was delivered in a low tone, implying caution.

"So-so," Hector replied vaguely.

Experience had taught him to trust nobody.

"But they're a cunning crowd behind it," he added.

"So they are," Welland agreed emphatically. "Not a doubt of it. That bunch in the Calgary country, now—"

"Is there a bunch working in the Calgary country?" asked Hector innocently.

"You know there is." Welland twinkled. "Guileless angel, ain't you? But, talking of whiskey—"

"Talkin' o' whiskey, are yah?" The trader's oily voice cut in suddenly. "You'll be able to talk o' whiskey for a long time, Sergeant, when you've signed this invoice!"

He winked meaningly at Welland, whose face for one moment betrayed surprise, then became intensely vigilant.

"What's this? What's this?" he exclaimed, half in jest, half in earnest, while his eyes flashed swiftly to the invoice.

Hector read and signed the piece of paper, which told him that Mr. John Adair, of Blenheim County, Ont., had recently shipped to him through Weatherton's chain of stores, evidently as a Christmas gift, one case of Scotch whiskey.

"Well, I'm shot!" Welland remarked. "I'll come an' see you when you've opened it, Hec'. How'll you get it into barracks?"

The last demand, with its veiled insinuation, irritated Hector. But he snubbed Welland by showing no concern.

"Bring it to my quarters next time you're over that way, Randall," he told the store-keeper.

"You're on, Sergeant," Randall leered, rolling his bleary eyes. "An' I hope to drink your health."

"You'll do it in water, then," Hector said quietly. "This whiskey goes to Mother Earth and no-one else."

"Wha-a-t?" Welland cried, amazed. "You're not—?"

"Yes, I am." Hector gathered up his whip and gloves. "I'm going to spill the lot of it, in Randall's presence, too. Nobody's going to say I'm a wholesale drinker myself and down on everyone else drinking."

"But Hec'! It came in a perfectly honest, legal way—"

"Can't help that. Shouldn't have come at all. I can take a drink with others, on the square or in the mess. But I'm not going to stock it myself. I've got too many people ready to take a crack at me and I won't run any chances."

"But Hec', it's a crime to waste—"

"No!" said Hector, real determination in the negative.

Welland drew back, defeated, shrugged his shoulders, and looked at the trader with a sneer.

"Hell!" he exclaimed audibly. "'Course he wants it for himself. That goody-goody stuff is bluff. That's the way with these zealots—no liquor, no! But that just applies to you—not me!"

The tone surprised Hector. He had not expected this thrust from Welland.

"Will you come over and see me get rid of that whiskey?" he flashed.

But Welland only laughed derisively.

"Well, Randall will be witness enough," Hector declared. "Think what you please, and be damned!"

With that, he clanked fiercely out of the store.

The trader exchanged glances with Welland, his florid face growing redder with suppressed delight.

III

Though John had sent the whiskey in a perfectly legitimate way, Hector could not use it, for the reason that, to do his work properly, he must keep up his reputation as an incorruptible enemy of liquor. If he gave way, his enemies would certainly adopt the cynical attitude that Hector, being able to get whiskey for himself whenever he pleased, had nothing to gain by winking at the operations of those less fortunate and so was zealous where he would otherwise have been slack. A better course than destroying the whiskey would have been to ship it straight back to John in Welland's presence; but Hector failed to think of this at the time.

In the late afternoon, Randall drove his sleigh into barracks.

"I got the case outside, Sergeant," he said. "Will I bring it in?"

"No," said Hector. "Dump it on the parade-ground."

Hector took an axe. They went out together.

"Why, Sergeant!" exclaimed Randall, in great alarm. "Yah ain't really goin'—? Ah, say, don't, Sergeant, don't! It's a sinful waste o' the gifts o' Providence, Sergeant—Ah!"

His voice rose to a shriek as Hector reduced the case to a pulp of splintered wood and broken glass.

"Now you tell anyone who ever mentions it what I do to private stock, Randall," said Hector, as he pitched the wreckage into the sleigh. "You understand. You've got to tell the truth. Savvy?"

"A'right, Sergeant, a'right!" Randall shrank back in alarm. "But it's an awful waste o' good Scotch!"

He drove off lamenting.

Hector's mistake had been in securing only one witness to the destruction of the whiskey. He was to pay for it later.

IV

Soon after this, Hector noticed a distinct falling off of the respectful regard held for him by the officers, the men, the civilians. They did not force the change upon him but they hinted at it in a thousand ways.

At a loss for an explanation, he did the wisest thing possible—ignored the change and went on his way in silence.

One day came light, when Inspector Denton summoned him and revealed the truth in a private interview.

"You sent for me, sir?" said Hector, entering the Inspector's sitting-room and saluting smartly.

Inspector Denton was a big man, much inclined to fatness. He had a ruddy face eloquent of good living, a drooping, luxuriant moustache, and an eye-glass which he hardly ever used. Ignorant recruits, judging by appearances, took him for a brainless martinet. As a matter of fact, the strength of a lion, the heart of a Viking and the endurance of a grizzly were hidden beneath his deceptive exterior and when action demanded those who doubted it were rapidly disillusioned.

The Inspector, as Hector entered, was seated by the stove, his tunic open, his feet in gaudy carpet slippers.

"Ah, Adair!" exclaimed the Inspector. "Er—just close the door, will you?"

Hector obeyed.

"I've been—ah—hearing tales about you, Adair," the Inspector began, composedly. "I don't like 'em. My advice is—er—if they're true—stop! I find it difficult to believe 'em, Adair. So I thought I'd talk it over quietly with you—er—alone."

"Tales about you!" Hector saw in a flash that the causes of the mysterious change were about to be revealed to him.

"Very good, sir," he said; and eagerly waited.

"Are they true?"

"I don't know what they are, sir."

"You don't, eh? Umph!"

The Inspector pondered. Then he looked at Hector again.

"Like me to tell you? Well—er—fact is, Adair, they say you're doing a lot of secret drinking, on cases sent from the East an' so on. Very foolish, Adair, if so. Must drink openly or not at all. Ah—makes your work in suppressing the traffic look so—so hypocritical, y'know—besides bringing the Force into disrepute. It's rather hard to explain what I mean but—er—you understand, eh?"

Hector's face crimsoned with passion.

"It's a lie!" he rapped fiercely. And he told the Inspector everything.

"I see!" said Denton thoughtfully. "I see! Well, we must kill this lie—er—immediately, Adair. It's done you a lot of harm—shaken people's confidence in you—er—considerably, very considerably. Even I was—er—a bit affected. Now let's see. How can we kill it, eh? How can we kill it?"

"I'll kill it, sir!" said Hector decidedly. "I'll kill it, all right!"

"Right you are, Adair! Good example, eh? Even stricter attention to duty—if that were possible—eh? But no violence. Anyway, that's all about it, s'far as I'm concerned. Damn' glad it wasn't true, Adair. Er—settle it quietly, eh? Damn' glad, Adair. Close the door, er—will you, when you go out?"

So this was the cause of the change in feeling! Obviously, it was the work of Randall or Welland, who must at least have started the rumour, whatever their part in its subsequent growth may have been! The story must be killed, the Inspector had said. Well, he would kill it, there and then!

Conscious of his innocence, Hector, for the first time since joining the Police, lost that crowning attribute, self-control.

On fire to avenge his honour, he left the Inspector's and went rapidly over to Weatherton's.

V

The door of the store was dashed open. Fifty startled men, settlers, constables, Indians and half-breeds, turned together towards it, leaving a lane to the counter.

Sergeant Adair came in. They all knew him—but not this Sergeant Adair. The quiet, friendly yet sternly restrained N.C.O. was gone and in his stead was a passionate giant, fists clenched, eyes like knives, lips set and cheeks aflame.

A hush fell on the crowd. It remained for Joe Welland to break it.

The rancher, in a big buffalo coat, was smoking a cigar at the counter. Turning with the rest, he looked at Hector coolly, though with genuine concern, and his voice cut evenly through the silence:

"What's the matter, Adair?"

Hector gripped himself before replying. He was joyfully conscious of the presence of many of his friends, assembled, as if by preordainment, to witness his vindication. There was MacFarlane, staring open-mouthed; Sergeant-Major Whittaker, by the stove, motionless in the act of pulling on his gloves, alert as a bird; Jim Jackson, master of ceremonies at the first Christmas celebration at the fort years before, pausing as he buttoned his fur coat for the trail; Martin Brent, seated on a sack of flour, pipe in mouth, stoically viewing the proceedings; Cranbrook—Corporal Cranbrook now; and a dozen others. For a moment Hector marshalled his words. Then he stepped swiftly into the centre of the room, the silent crowd shrinking before him.

"This is the matter!" he burst out furiously. "Which of you two started these lies about me—you—or you?"

And he pointed an accusing finger, first at Welland, then at Randall.

Deathly silence came again. Men looked at one another. Welland gaped.

"What d'you mean, Hec'? No-one's——

"Oh, yes, they have! Someone's been spreading tales that I've been getting secret whiskey from the East. Don't deny it! I know positively the story's gone 'round for weeks. Am I right, boys?—am I right?"

He flung the appeal to the crowd. They growled assent.

"That's right—that's true."

"Do you hear them?" Hector cried. "There's proof, isn't it? Now, which of you two began it? You know, Welland, that I had a case sent unexpectedly from the East. Randall knows it. You know I said I was going to destroy it. Randall saw me smash it with an axe that same afternoon. Now, no one else in the world knew that whiskey had come to me! Then, which of you spread the story? That's what I want to know."

The crowd waited breathlessly.

Welland calmly flicked the ash from his cigar and smiled.

"Say, you can take this as straight," he asserted. "I've said nothing. If anyone's told any yarns, it's Randall there, not me."

And he glanced with stern contempt at the store-keeper.

Randall started, staring with alarm and consternation.

"Well, say!" he shrilled. "For God's sake, Welland——"

"You shut up!" flashed Welland. Then, quietly, to Hector: "That's your man, Adair."

Hector turned quickly to the crowd.

"Did this man start the rumour?" he demanded, pointing at Randall.

For a moment no-one answered. Fear of a tempest held them silent.

"Did he?"

"I heard it first from him, Sergeant."

The voice, pleasant, careless but assured, was Cranbrook's.

That broke the spell. A chorus of "So did I," "I did, too," rolled solemnly through the crowd.

Hector's fury broke.

MacFarlane raised a husky shout as a dozen bystanders threw themselves on Hector:

"What'you going to do? What'you going to do?"

Jim Jackson rushed into action, shouting, "No, Adair—no!"

Then came a babble:

"Hold him! Hold him!" and a storm of curses——

At the stove Whittaker still stood motionless but smiling quietly——

And Hector burst out of the crowd like a lion from a thicket of spears, grim, silent, deadly. He tossed Jackson and MacFarlane aside with a great sweep of his arm—the powers of twenty men added to his own giant strength in that moment. The trader's frenzied shriek, "Sergeant—for the love of Christ!" he did not heed at all. Seizing Randall in a grip that brought a scream to his lips, he dragged him swiftly across the counter. The scattered crowd closed in. Seeing them, he swung the trader like a flail through the air, dashing them off their feet. In the cleared space, he shook his victim as if he were a sawdust dummy.

"You dog! You dog!" they heard him crying.

Once more the crowd rushed, to save Hector from murder.

"Get back, damn you! He's mine!" Hector roared, pinning the maddened Randall against the counter and staving them off.

"Say you're a liar, you cur! You swine!" he gasped, "Say it or I'll kill you—I'll kill you———"

"I am! I am!" sobbed Randall. "Sergeant—Sergeant———"

"Let him go, Hec'! Let him go!"

MacFarlane's voice gave Hector back his sanity. But, shifting his grip, he tossed the trader, screaming, above his head and held him there, his eyes roving furiously 'round the room.

Then, taking ten great strides, he hurled him crashing but unhurt into a pile of hardware.

"I could kill you!" was in his mind. But instead he said, "Lie there, you dog; lie there!"

Ignoring the crowd utterly—it parted in his path with awed silence—he went to the door, flung it wide open.

The crash of the heavy portal slamming to aroused the crowd to tumult.

VI

Within twenty-four hours the whiskey rumour was as dead as a last year's calendar and Hector was back upon his pedestal.

Mention of his name thenceforward produced this invariable comment:

"Play straight with Adair. He's an easy-goin' bird, but a ring-tailed devil when he's roused!"